PUFFIN BOOKS

THE CALL AND OTHER STORIES

Robert Westall was born in 1929 on Tyneside, where he grew up during the Second World War. He went to Tynemouth High School and then studied Fine Art at Durham University, and Sculpture at the Slade School of Fine Art in London. He worked for more than twenty-five years as an Art teacher in the North of England. He was also a Branch Director of the Samaritans, a journalist and an antiques dealer.

His first novel for children, *The Machine Gunners*, was published by Macmillan in 1975. It was an instant success and was awarded the Carnegie Medal. He won the Carnegie again in 1982 for *The Scarecrows*, (the first writer to win the Medal twice), the Smarties Prize in 1989 for *Blitzcat*, and the *Guardian* award in 1991 for *The Kingdom by the Sea*. Between 1985 and his death in 1993, he retired to devote himself to his writing.

Robert Westall

THE CALL
AND OTHER STORIES

PUFFIN BOOKS

To Nitoko Takisawa of Iwate
my Japanese correspondent

PUFFIN BOOKS

Published by the Penguin Group
Penguin Books Ltd, 27 Wrights Lane, London W8 5TZ, England
Penguin Books USA Inc., 375 Hudson Street, New York, New York 10014, USA
Penguin Books Australia Ltd, Ringwood, Victoria, Australia
Penguin Books Canada Ltd, 10 Alcorn Avenue, Toronto, Ontario, Canada M4V 3B2
Penguin Books (NZ) Ltd, 182–190 Wairau Road, Auckland 10, New Zealand

Penguin Books Ltd, Registered Offices: Harmondsworth, Middlesex, England

First published by Viking 1989
Published in Penguin Books 1991
Reissued in Puffin Books 1995
1 3 5 7 9 10 8 6 4 2

Printed in England by Clays Ltd, St Ives plc
Filmset in Monophoto Photina

Contents

Woman and Home

The house caught him, the first time he played truant from school.

Playing truant wasn't a habit. This was the first time. The trouble was, he was new at the school, and not fitting in. He'd come from a county grammar, and this was a city comprehensive. He had a posh accent he wasn't able to hide. Anyway, why should he? It was his voice.

He was bullied; but he didn't bully easy. He was tall and thin, but quick and not soft. When Brewster tried twisting his arm, he gave Brewster a very bloody nose. That should have finished it, especially as Brewster was far from heroic in defeat. It *would* have finished it, at his old grammar school.

But this was a city comprehensive, and not a well-run one. Brewster went to his Head of Year to complain, and it was the victim who got the telling-off.

'We don't hold with physical violence in this school,' said the Head. 'We find talking things out peacefully is better.'

He shook hands with Brewster in front of the Head. But afterwards Brewster was not inclined to talk things out peacefully; he summoned his gang. It never came to fists again. No, it was endless little things that weren't worth reporting. Like being tripped-up in the corridor; or having your bag snatched from under your arm, and tipped out under the feet of the trampling herd. Or having 'London Pouf' scrawled on your locker-door with lipstick, or having your trousers dumped under the shower if you weren't back first from games.

They never seemed to tire of it. And after a month came the

morning he just couldn't face any more of it. He turned away back towards the city centre.

He solved one problem, and immediately a lot of others landed on his head. Had any of his class seen him duck down the side-street? They would certainly report *him* to the form-master.

And here was one of them coming towards him up the side-street now . . .

He ducked away like a rabbit, into an even more ramshackle side-street, lined with rusty corrugated sheds in a sea of rose-bay willowherb, and realized the city centre wasn't for him today. It would be full of teachers nipping out to do a bit of shopping in their free period, governors who would recognize his uniform, his mum's new friends and neighbours . . .

So he wandered the back-streets; until it started to rain. Pretty heavily. Where on earth could he *go*? Mum only worked part time, and she would be home all day, doing the washing and ironing. They knew him at the library, the bowling-alley was shut; there was no cinema matineé till two o'clock, and *they'd* just ring school anyway.

The only place in the world was a derelict shed with the door hanging off its hinges. He slipped in like a thief. The floor was wet mud, a pattern of footprints filling with water from a big puddle in the middle. There were two big blue oil-drums lying on their sides, and a heap of black and white ash, where somebody had tried setting fire to the end wall. Somebody else had scrawled, in huge letters of yellow chalk, BANANA-LEGS IS A BUMMER.

Banana-legs was what they called the Head, because he braced his legs back tensely while waiting for something like silence to fall in assembly.

The evil-doers had been here before him; this was where *they* came when they were playing truant and it rained.

He was one of them now. He was sure some kid would have reported him. The Head would ring his mum. Trouble with Dad who was already worried sick about his new job . . .

He wished he was back in school. School might be hell, but

it was better than *this*. He looked at his watch; an age seemed to have passed; but it was only twenty past nine. Soon, they'd be coming out of assembly. If he ran, could he slip in with them to first lesson?

But he knew even if he ran like mad he'd never make it. He'd arrive wet and sweating in the middle of the lesson, to face questions and jeers.

The rain fell heavier, making a noise like machine-guns on the tin roof. What could he *do*?

First lesson was English. In a desperate attempt to be a law-abiding citizen, he got out his English book, sat on a blue oil-drum and tried to read. But it was too dark. And drops of water from the leaking roof began falling on his head.

The quality of the light changed. He looked up, to see a cat peering in the door. A cheerful-looking black cat, with a white bib. It seemed a godsend . . . he was good at making friends with cats. He held out his hand, called gently to it.

It gave him a look of sheer contempt and vanished.

Even the cat didn't want him . . .

He packed up his books in a frenzy; as he did so, his English exercise-book fell into the mud. Open. At the English essay he'd spent two hours on last night. A *good* essay, because he *liked* English.

He fastened his bag and ran out of that dreadful place like a mad thing; just wanting to get away. Anywhere.

That was when the house caught him.

It was the sun shining on the wet back of his neck that brought him to his senses. He looked around in surprise. It had stopped raining; the sky was blue, with only a few little friendly fluffy clouds. And he was utterly lost. But still he was afraid somebody might drive past in a car and see him. They said the Heads of Year spent half their days driving round the town looking for truants out of school. He *must* get under cover.

There was a high, overgrown privet hedge. A giant, obscene privet hedge like a young forest, ten feet high. And a double white gate. Half the gate was open. It drooped into the gravel as if it hadn't been moved in years. The paint was peeling off, leaving the wood beneath dark and soggy. Beyond, a worn gravel drive wound round to the left. There were tall thin fronds of grass growing out of the drive, all over. Dry and dead, last year's grass. Nobody must have gone up that drive for ages. It was *inviting*. Well, at least the passing cars wouldn't see him . . .

Even Brewster might've warned him. But Brewster wasn't there.

It was a funny garden. He helped Dad with the garden at home, so he soon spotted just how funny it was. Nobody had touched it for years; but it was OK. It hadn't turned into a jungle. He could see where weeds had tried to grow; but the weeds had died. They lay like shrivelled little pale corpses, though it was high summer. Whereas the garden plants and flowers were doing fine. Mind you, they needed pruning; the roses had put out branches ten feet high, that waved in the warm breeze like crazy fishing-rods. But they were doing OK.

Perhaps that should've warned him, too. But he passed up the formal garden, suddenly happy and peaceful and feeling at home. Up the stone steps, between the mossy pair of urns, up to the statue and the lily pond, where the white flowers were just breaking the surface, and goldfish big as herring swam in the green depths. He wondered what the goldfish fed on . . .

He looked up, and saw the house.

He had to squint at it, because the sun was above it, and the sun was also reflecting up from the dark water of the lily pond.

He couldn't make out if anyone was at home or not. There was no smoke coming from the white chimneys, but then it was summer.

There were no broken windows, or slates off the roof. There were curtains at the windows, and stuff inside.

On the other hand, there was a white verandah with wistaria growing up the pillars. Lumps of the wistaria had grown out uncontrolled, and been tugged free of their wires by the wind, and hung in great loose clumps, swaying, as nobody who loved plants would've allowed. Nobody in their right mind would've allowed. They swayed crazily, dangerously.

The other odd thing was the half-bricks lying on the paths between him and the house. Not many, but placed temptingly, tempting you to hurl them into the lily pond, or through the glass of the frail conservatory.

The temptation *annoyed* him; because he was not that sort of person. It wasn't that he was a goody-goody, or teacher's pet. It was because he *liked* lily ponds and conservatories and old houses . . . So he carefully picked the half-bricks from the paths, and tucked them away out of sight, before they tempted somebody else.

In the same way, when he reached the verandah, he couldn't help fastening back the wistaria inside its wires as best he could, and neatly pruning off the rest with his pocket-knife. It seemed to *want* to be done, somehow . . .

And then a door banged, round the corner of the verandah. He stood, paralysed with the knowledge that somebody lived here after all; blushing from head to foot with embarrassment that they must have been watching him, fiddling with their wistaria. Such enormous *cheek* . . . he waited, wild-eyed, trembling.

But the minutes passed, and nobody came. In the end, he moved, his legs stiff with tension. Round the corner . . .

There was a door. A double door, with glass panes in the top. One half was open. But as he watched, it swung closed in the wind, with the same bang. Then, in the next gust of wind, it swung open again.

And closed.

Then open again. The paint on the door was peeling off in great curls, like the paint on the gate. As the door slammed open and shut, great flakes fell off, to join flakes already lying on the verandah. It said quite clearly to him that nobody had lived there for ages. But if it was allowed to go on slamming in the wind, sooner or later the glass would break, the door would come off its hinges, the rain would get in.

He walked forward to shut the door safely.

And saw the huge heap of letters lying on the doormat inside. Like they'd found at home, when they came back from a fortnight's holiday. He peered down at them. The ones at the bottom were browning with age and rain and mingled with brown leaves that had blown in, but the ones on the top looked quite new. Again, it offended him; it was a breach in the sensible world. He leaned through, and gathered them up, crouching on his heels and swaying dangerously, for he had a reluctance to put a foot inside. Then he retired to the fence of the verandah and sorted them into order by postmark. The oldest were over a year old, but some were only a week. Most of it was junk, addressed to 'The Occupier' but there was one addressed to 'Miss Nadine Marriner' in a small, mean, spidery hand. And somehow the name made him shudder, in spite of the warmth of the sun on his back. Miss Nadine Marriner – it had a thin spiteful sound, he thought.

There were a couple of elastic bands round some of the letters. He used them to make the whole thing into a neat bundle. But what to do with the bundle? He looked through the glass panes and saw a hall table, and a grandfather clock.

Well then, put them all on the hall table, slam the door shut properly, so it wouldn't blow open again, and that was *that*. Somehow, although he liked the garden a lot, he didn't like the house so much. It looked dark inside, after the sunny garden.

He stepped in, and put the letters on the table. Looked at the grandfather clock. He sometimes went round the antique fairs with Dad. Dad liked to buy up old stopped clocks cheap, mend them, and sell them at a profit. Notes in your hand and not a word to the Inland Revenue.

This clock was stopped. But he could also see it was a very good one, with a silvered brass face, and brass tops to the columns, and a little brass eagle on top. Even with the dead leaves gathered in a drift round its base, it looked what Dad called a two-thousand-pound clock . . . He opened the door in the base, and looked inside. The pendulum was properly hung, the weights in place, but run down right on to the floor. That was why the clock had stopped. He reached automatically for the shelf where keys were usually kept. The key was there. Unthinking, he put it into the winding-holes, and wound up the heavy weights and swung the pendulum.

Immediately the clock began to tick, a slow stately beat, that was a comfort to the ear. It seemed gently to bring the whole house alive.

Then suddenly, without warning, it chimed. Loud and long, it struck ten, though the hands pointed to half past two. He knew he shouldn't be alarmed. When clocks wound down, the chime sometimes got out of synch, as Dad said. But the chimes were so *loud* and triumphant; as if the clock was telling the whole house, the whole world, that he had come. He suddenly felt he had done something irrevocable. He turned to run . . .

He heard the door slam shut in the wind, behind him.

Oh, well, open, shut, open, shut.

But when he pulled at the brass handle, green with lack of polishing, he found the lock had really worked this time. The door really was shut. And, what's more, struggle as he might, he couldn't get it open again.

Well, he told himself bravely, there will be other doors; or windows at a pinch, if they weren't painted up solid. He moved forward into the house, among the shadows. Outside, the sun had gone in . . .

He had a funny desire, every few paces, to stop and listen for other footsteps. Especially footsteps upstairs. That locked door made a difference. Before, one sound and he could have taken to his heels, and been out of the house and out of the garden in less than a minute. Now he was . . .

A prisoner. No longer free. If somebody came, he would have to do what they said . . .

The sooner he got out of here, the better.

He went into the first room with an open door. It seemed

less cheeky. Less dangerous than trying one of the closed doors.

This was obviously the kitchen. Huge cold black kitchen range, and a battered electric cooker that must have been 1950s. Stone-flagged floor, with beetles scurrying away into the dark corners. The sink was full of dirty dishes, on to which the cold tap dripped, its sound quarrelling with the ticking of the clock that had followed him in. Every work-surface was covered with an intricate clutter, like a spider's web to catch the eye. He got a feel of Miss Nadine Marriner's mind, somehow. A muddled, devious, cluttered mind. He didn't like it. His mum kept their kitchen spotlessly tidy.

But the huge pine table in the middle of the kitchen held different kinds of things. A packet of cigarettes, with one taken out, smoked, and left as a trampled-out stub on the floor. A tin, with three crude rough-looking cigarettes inside, that smelt funny when he sniffed them. Reefers?

A bottle of whisky, half-empty. And a glass with a thin damp brown stain on the bottom.

He sniffed without touching. Yes, it was whisky all right.

Again, he was tempted. But he'd tried whisky, and hated the taste. And his first and only cigarette had made him sick. Besides, he didn't know where they'd been.

He left them alone.

He looked under the table. There was a huge dirty bundle there; a sleeping-bag wrapped round what looked like trousers and sweaters, with an enamel mug attached by a length of coarse white string.

A tramp's bundle. A man-tramp, from the smell of it.

So now he had a tramp to worry about, as well. An old lady was one thing. But a tramp who probably stole whisky and reefers was a lot more scary.

C'mon, let's get out of here. Quick. He moved swiftly to the kitchen door. Undid the bolts, top and bottom. But it was locked as well, with a huge old-fashioned lock. And the key wasn't in it. He searched the cluttered work-surface in vain, feeling he was wasting time he could ill afford.

Well, other rooms then. With a verandah, there were bound to be french windows.

The next room did have french windows.

And a dog lying down next to them, asleep. Probably the tramp's dog. If he tried to get out through the french windows, it might wake up and bark, or even attack him. The tramp would come. From upstairs. He kept having this funny feeling there was somebody upstairs.

He studied the dog carefully. It didn't look dangerous. It was a small brown mongrel, with floppy ears. Oh, he could deal with that. He tiptoed forwards, trying not to wake it. Reached the french windows, and twisted the handle.

It didn't open. He saw with despair the empty keyhole. Almost felt the dog reaching to bite his ankle. It must have heard, must have wakened.

But it still lay there. It lay there, still. *Too* still. Its belly wasn't going up and down. It wasn't *breathing*.

It must be *dead*. He looked down at it in horror. It still looked just . . . asleep. Comfortably asleep. There was no smell or maggots or any kind of nastiness, like fur falling off. Not like the dogs you saw floating drowned in the river . . .

He *had* to touch it. He didn't want to, but he *had* to.

It moved dryly, all of a piece, like a statue.

It was a stuffed dog. A real dog, real skin and fur, that had died and been stuffed. Nothing to do with any tramp. This had cost a lot of money. It must have been Miss Nadine Marriner's pet, that had died. She must have had it stuffed and gone on living with it.

What a crazy thing to do, living with a dead stuffed pet!

Then he wished he hadn't thought that. It wasn't nice to think Miss Nadine Marriner was crazy. But it explained the open door, and the leaves blowing in on priceless antiques, and the pile of unopened letters. He listened. Listened especially for ceilings creaking, which would mean somebody moving, upstairs. But there was just silence, and the ticking of the clock.

He looked longingly outside, through the glass of the french windows. There, at the end of the garden, was the drooping white gate. Beyond, cars would be passing. Far off, his class would be having their break. He could break the glass, get out that way. The sun was shining out there again.

But it wouldn't mean just breaking one pane of glass. It would mean breaking the french windows.

And he couldn't do that.

Well, there were plenty more rooms. Get on with it. You're just being silly. This is Monday morning the 3rd of October 1988, and Mum is at home doing the washing. What could possibly happen?

As he turned to go back to the door, he saw the rocking-chair. A big American rocker with a green upholstered back and seat. The upholstery was old, worn and greasy. And it seemed to bear the marks of a thin body, worn into it with time. There was a hooky mat beneath it, worn through to the canvas where two feet had pressed. There was a bag hanging on one arm of the chair, a cracked plastic bag, with a trail of tangled grey knitting dangling from it. On the other side of the chair, on the dusty carpet, was a cup and saucer, with a dry brown stain on the bottom.

He just knew this was where Miss Nadine Marriner had sat all day, knitting something the dullest grey colour imaginable. She was so much *there* that he gave a little humble apologetic bob of his head, and said absurdly, 'I'm sorry. I'm just going. When I can find a way out.'

The moment he spoke, he knew it was a mistake. Speaking to the chair made Miss Nadine Marriner more real in his mind. He could imagine her, now. Very thin, with gold-rimmed spectacles and grey hair pulled back in a bun, and knobbled veined thin hands, knitting, knitting. He couldn't *move*, for looking at the chair. He couldn't make his legs work, standing facing the empty chair, with the stuffed dog at his back.

Then with a yell like a feeble war-cry, he moved and leapt past the chair. As he passed it, he must have caught it with his sleeve. For when he glanced back from the doorway, it was rocking, rocking.

Frantic, now, he tried other doors. All were locked. And he could tell from trying to force the handles that they were very solid old Victorian doors. And from under one came the foulest smell he had ever smelt. A smell of utter rottenness. Like the time they came back from holiday, and the freezer had broken down, and the smell of that joint of pork Mum had been keeping for their return . . .

But he consoled himself that that door was plain, and next to the kitchen. Must be the pantry door. Some meat must have been left, and gone rotten inside. He thought he heard the buzz of a bluebottle, through the thick woodwork.

But he could've been imagining it. He knew he was in a very odd mood, one he'd never been in before. His body was shaky, his mind all whirly. He was starting to be silly and imagine things. He must get a grip on himself.

He must go upstairs. Look for keys, he told himself. So he wouldn't have to start smashing his way out . . . But he knew he was kidding himself.

Upstairs was calling him. He didn't want to go up there; he didn't want the shock of opening any more doors, of walking into rooms where he didn't know what he might see. The tramp asleep, snoring. Suddenly opening his eyes. Or Miss Nadine Marriner, standing watching him. Or Miss Nadine Marriner dead in her bed.

He hovered piteously in the hall, looking out through the glass in the door at the sunlit garden. Again, he contemplated smashing the glass, knocking out every sharp edge and crawling through to freedom. But suppose somebody came, while he was doing it . . .

Finally, he turned, and slowly began to climb the stairs. The stair-carpet was thick, but old and grey and full of dust. The dust shot up in clouds from his feet. Hung golden in the shafts of sunlight streaming down from the window on the landing above. The dust of Miss Nadine Marriner, creeping, sweet and sour, into his body through his nostrils, so he wanted to stop breathing.

And the sun was shining down the stairs so brightly, he

couldn't see if there was anybody standing at the top of the stairs, waiting for him.

But there wasn't. There was just the window. It was clear in the middle (though very much spattered by dirty rain) but blue and red stained-glass round the edges. Through it, he could see what appeared to be the kitchen garden. Again, not much in the way of weeds, but cabbages sprouting to a great height with yellow strings of flowers. And beyond the garden, quite far off, a kind of summer-house with glass windows.

And the window in the door of it was broken.

And through the jagged hole, he could see what looked like a flat bloated figure, half lying, half sitting inside. He might have thought it was a bundle of dark old clothes, except he could see the head, and a blurred sort of face, with dark holes for eyes, looking up at him in a rather pleading way. It gave him quite a turn, though it must have been fifty or sixty feet away, just sitting there, staring up at this window.

Then he realized it must be a made-up stuffed figure, a Guy Fawkes or a scarecrow, because the face was all weird colours, green and purple, and the eyes were just holes.

He had enough worries, without scarecrows stored in summer-houses. Find a key, and get out!

The first three doors were locked. Again he smelt, more faintly, the smell of rotting pork; but he thought it must be drifting upstairs from the larder. For it was *very* much fainter.

The last door was half open. But the room beyond was dim, as if the curtains were drawn. He hovered, listening. No sound at all; except the ticking of the clock, coming up the stairs behind. He sniffed. There was a very strong smell of old lady. Lavender and powder, old sweat and the sickly sweetness of age. He felt pulled forwards, as the receding waves had tried to suck him out to sea last summer. But he fought against it, now. As if he knew once he was sucked into that room, he would never come out again.

And then, downstairs, the clock struck eleven. The clang seemed to fill the whole house. And it was as if it was announcing his presence outside that door.

He was caught. He had to walk in.

There was a figure standing straight opposite him, in the gloom of the drawn curtains. A figure that watched him with eyes that glared out of a white face, standing stock-still.

It was no bigger than he himself. It made no move to attack, standing with its arms by its sides. It looked . . .

Hopeless, helpless, drowned in the green gloom.

He half raised an arm, to ward off the terrified glare.

The figure in turn raised its arm.

And then he saw it was himself; caught in the long mirror of a wardrobe. But lost, drowned, frozen as if under green ice.

He tried to force a laugh; it failed, making a weird mad sound in that dim silent room. But it released him to move.

He swung round to look behind the door, where the bed would be . . .

The bed was made, pulled flat and tight. Nothing to be afraid of there. He looked under the bed; nothing but the dim shine of a white chamber-pot. He let his eyes pan to the left. A chair with a heap of old lady's dark clothes piled up on it. Another mirror, above a dressing-table, as cluttered as the kitchen work-surfaces downstairs. Miss Nadine Marriner's, without a doubt. Then a tall dark chest of drawers, with half the drawers pulled open, and pale female things hanging out.

Then the big white marble fireplace, and above it . . .

Miss Nadine Marriner stared down at him.

Larger than life. Seated in the rocking-chair from downstairs, with her knobbled veined hands clutching the wooden arms with a grip that said 'Mine, mine, *mine*!' She looked exactly as he had imagined her, when he first saw the rocking-chair. Tall, very bony, with gold-rimmed spectacles and her grey hair pulled back tight in a bun.

A portrait. A picture in oils, in a huge gilt frame. Just a huge oil-painting. But how could he have known so exactly what she would look like, before he saw the portrait?

And why did the face stare at him so, the eyes seeming to burn right through him, as if she was alive? Why did it make him feel so small, so helpless, so . . . obedient? Why did her presence seem to fill the whole room, the whole house? And why did he stand so submissive, waiting for her to . . .

Speak. He was waiting for her to speak; to give him orders. To obey her every whim, even as he saw, without hope, the cruelty in her, the lack of any sort of kindness or mercy.

He waited.

And then he saw the picture was a little crooked; it sloped down a little to the right.

He must set it straight. Slowly he walked up to it, closer and closer to those claw hands, those piercing eyes.

He tried to straighten the picture by grasping the two bottom corners. But the picture wouldn't move; it seemed stuck to the wall. He tried to pull it away, towards him.

As it moved and straightened, something fell down from behind it, bounced on the marble top of the mantelpiece, and fell among the soot-splashes that the rain had left on the green tiles of the hearth.

A thick brown letter.

Well, he couldn't just leave it there, getting dirty among the soot. He picked it up, and read the writing on the envelope.

TO THE FINDER.

That was *him*. And he was in no state to disobey the tall, spiky, spidery handwriting of Miss Nadine Marriner.

Inside was another envelope, and a note.

The note said, DELIVER THIS BY HAND TO THE AD-DRESS ON THE ENVELOPE.

The envelope was addressed to a firm of solicitors in the city centre. It was open, and he could not help being curious. He looked up at the piercing eyes of Miss Nadine Marriner, and strangely they did not forbid him.

He opened the envelope, and unfolded the large stiff piece of paper. It was headed, THE LAST WILL AND TESTAMENT OF NADINE MARRINER, DECEASED.

He shuddered a little, and read on.

I AM DEAD. HAVE NO DOUBT ABOUT THAT. DO

NOT LOOK FOR MY CORPSE. YOU WILL NEVER
FIND IT. I AM IN A VERY SAFE PLACE.

BUT I LEAVE MY HOUSE, LANDS, AND ALL I
AM POSSESSED OF TO THE BEARER OF THIS
LETTER. I HAVE FOUND HIM HONEST AND
TRUSTWORTHY. HE WILL CARE FOR THE HOUSE
AND MY POSSESSIONS NOW I AM DEAD. HE
GETS IT ONLY ON CONDITION THAT HE SELLS
NOTHING, BUT LIVES IN THIS HOUSE, AND
KEEPS IT AS IT IS AND IN GOOD REPAIR AS
LONG AS HE SHALL LIVE.

AS FOR THE OTHERS WHO CAME, THE THIEVES
WHO TRIED TO STEAL, THE VANDALS WHO CAME
TO SMASH AND BURN, FIND THEM WHERE YOU
MAY AND BURY THEM WHERE YOU WILL. THEY
BROUGHT THEIR DEATH UPON THEMSELVES.

There was more, and signatures at the bottom. Miss Nadine
Marriner and two others he couldn't read.

The phrases hammered through his head. 'They brought
their death upon themselves . . . Find them where you may and
bury them where you will.'

He remembered the bloated green-faced scarecrow who had
glared up at him so pleadingly from the broken glass of the
summer-house. The awful smell in the room downstairs . . .
The whole house was a *trap*. He remembered the half-bricks
he had been tempted to throw in the lily pond, and at the frail
conservatory. The whisky and the cigarettes and the reefers
on the kitchen table. How many more traps?

And he knew she *was* still here. In the house. He had a
weird feeling she was behind that tomb-like marble fireplace,
still sitting upright in her chair, her hands clutched on the
arms, saying, 'Mine, mine, *mine*.' The whole house was full of
her. It was as if she had moved out of her tall frail body, into
the bricks and mortar, the glass and wood, the very soil itself,
poisoning the intruding weeds . . . What had the huge goldfish
fed on, to stay alive all this time?

There was no way out. He was trapped, finished. He must obey her, or he would never get out of here. And if he obeyed her, he would be caught up with her in a bargain, till the day he died . . .

And then he remembered the pile of letters on the doormat. The postman must have walked up the path nearly every day, and walked out again, untouched.

Because he was innocent. Because he was just delivering letters, whistling to himself, thinking about something else.

It gave him a little bit of courage. Enough to put everything back in the big envelope, and to say firmly, 'No thanks,' and to lift the portrait and tuck the letter back where it had come from.

He was frightened it might fall out again; with a dreadful insistence; as a dreadful warning.

But it stayed where it was. So he went while the going was good. Down the dust-laden stairs, to the front door. Through its glass he could see his schoolbag lying on the verandah, where he'd left it, what seemed like half a lifetime ago.

He put his hand on the dark-green brass of the door handle and tried it.

It turned first time, and he grabbed his bag and was off the verandah, tearing past the goldfish pond, down the steps between the urns, and out through the white gate.

He was still running when he heard a voice bellow.

'*HIGGINSON!*'

He stopped because that was his name. He had a feeling that the voice had been bellowing it for some time.

He was in the city centre, between the McDonald's and the video shop. He had no idea what streets he had run down, what streets he must have crossed, though he had a vague memory of car-horns hooting.

'Higginson? Where the hell do you think you are going? What's got into you, lad?'

It was Toddser Todd, Head of Third Year, glaring at him through the wound-down window of his Ford Fiesta, his red face clashing horribly with his ginger hair.

He didn't like Toddser much; didn't trust him. But at that moment, he felt like flinging his arms around his neck. But he only went over, and leaned against the car's bonnet, shaking all over.

'Get in,' said Toddser. 'You're in trouble, real trouble. This will have to go to the Head. You kids think you can get away with murder . . .'

He got in, and held his bag tight on his knee, so that Toddser wouldn't see how much his legs were shaking. But Toddser wasn't interested. He was still cruising the town centre, peering down every side-street they came to, looking for other truants, and at the same time mumbling the same old crap about order and discipline that he must mumble to all the kids he caught. But you could tell he was pleased to have caught somebody; you could tell he enjoyed the game.

'You're in *real* trouble,' went on Toddser like a tape-recording. 'You don't know what real trouble is like, tili now . . .'

'I won't do it again, sir,' he said, with a great deal of fervour. So that Toddser, halted at a traffic-light, stared at him as if he was seeing him for the first time and said,

'You sound as if you really mean it.'

Then the lights changed, and Toddser drove back to school, and he closed his eyes and relaxed into the paradise of the real trouble to come. Knowing he could never find that white gate again. Even if he *tried*.

Uncle Otto at
Denswick Park

'Uncle Otto's coming to stay,' said Mum. 'For a fortnight. He's doing some work in the Fitzwilliam.'

'Oh, good,' I said. With mixed feelings. It's not that I don't like Uncle Otto. But he's quite liable to trip over his own feet and fall downstairs. And since he's six foot three, and as wide as a house, there'd not be much furniture left where he hit the bottom.

Don't think he's stupid. He's only Professor Otto Altdorfer, of the Courtauld Institute, and the biggest brain on eighteenth-century art in Europe. And don't think he's not kind and generous. The first time I met him, I'd just unpacked my first camera.

'Keen on photography, *hein?*' says Uncle Otto. 'May I see it?'

He immediately dropped it. Beyond repair. And just as immediately ordered a taxi for us into Cambridge and bought me the best camera in the shop. And a gadget-bag. And about ten rolls of film.

'Oh, Otto, you shouldn't have,' said Mum, when we got home. 'You've spent a fortune on him ...'

'A fortune I have,' said Uncle Otto sadly, 'but no son of my own.'

He's been married twice, but it didn't work. He must be no better with women than he is with cameras. He once had a new secretary he couldn't get on with. All sorts of funny things started happening in his office block. The lights and heating kept turning themselves on, on their own, in the middle of the day, in mid-summer. Telephones kept ringing non-stop, but when they answered, there was never anybody there. Finally, they reckoned they'd tracked it down to the girl, who was sort of poltergeisting the place. As soon as they sacked her, the disturbances stopped. But Uncle Otto was very sorry for her – said it wasn't her fault. Gave her a marvellous reference, got her a new job and gave her three months pay in compensation. He said it was the least he could do. As I said, he's crazy-generous.

He's very shy. He has these big hornrim spectacles and jutting nose, and when he loses his temper they make him look very fierce. But behind his spectacles his eyes are big and dark and soft; they peep out at you like a little deer's. He'll never look you in the eye, and yet a more honest man never lived. I expect he only glares at people when he's angry; and he only gets angry when someone breaks something beautiful that belongs to the eighteenth century.

Once, he tried and tried and tried to save a little gateway in London. But he failed, though he knows everybody famous and has even been to dinner at 10 Downing Street. And on the morning when the bulldozers moved in, he went berserk and started a fight with the site-foreman. Flailing like a windmill he was, and just one blow caught the foreman and knocked him unconscious. When he came up in court, the character-witnesses in his defence sounded like a page from *Who's Who*. He got bound over to keep the peace, because the magistrates said he had been driven by an ungovernable passion, and he'd never been in court before. Even the site-foreman shook hands with him, and said he'd missed a great career in the ring. Everybody gets very fond of Uncle Otto.

But the eighteenth century is his life. Mum isn't really his niece; she was one of his students at the Courtauld. She says he's an obsessional. He once finished a lecture on Sir John Soane early, at two minutes to six. All the students were stretching and picking up their notebooks, when he started a new two-minute lecture on John Carr of York. Doesn't believe in wasting a second. All the same, he had a nice sense of humour, she says, which made the students like him. Once flashed a picture of Blenheim Palace on the screen and said, 'Perhaps you will like this picture of my country cottage ...'

Anyway, the trouble started when we went to pick him up from the station in the car. (He doesn't drive; failed his test ten times, which does help to keep death off the road.) We'd moved house to Denswick Park since he'd last been to see us. Now Denswick Park was once a Georgian stately home. But it got into the hands of the Army in the war, and was then passed on to a nationalized industry, who knocked the tops off all the chimneys and built a lot of prefab huts on to it. And then some developers got it, and let the house rot, because they wanted to build an estate of four-bedroom executive bungalows in the grounds. So all that's really left is the big wall round it, the gate-pillars and one wing of the house that's been left as the estate sports and social club.

The moment he sees the wall, Uncle Otto puts a hand as big as a cabbage on Mum's shoulder and says in an awed voice, 'Stop, Marjorie.'

And Mum stops; right there on the double yellow lines. And the whole car feels like we're in church.

'A crinkle-crankle wall,' says Otto in hushed tones. Because it's a wall that keeps curving in and out, all the way round. 'Such craftsmanship; such expense! What *can* the house be like? I had not heard of it. Who is the owner? I must ring him!'

Mum is a coward. She turned pale. She hadn't the heart to say anything. She drove up to the gate. And again Uncle Otto said, 'Stop, Marjorie!' Because those gate-posts are *really* something. Twenty feet high, with super great lions on top, holding shields in their paws.

'*Mein Gott*,' says Otto, 'why has no one written of this place?' He grabbed a little notebook out of his pocket, and began scribbling frantically. Then Mum drove through; and he saw the rows of four-bedroom executive bungalows. He turned pale; his beaky nose quivered. His great hands clenched. I was glad this site-foreman had been gone two years, and there was only old Fred Streeter mowing his front lawn ...

'What *criminal* has done this thing? He should be shot!' Then he added, 'Where is the great house?'

Silently, Mum drove him to the sports and social club. With its chimneys cut off. And a glass and aluminium lounge-solarium built on to what's left of the six-bayed Georgian front. And the tennis courts occupying what's left of a terrace designed by John Nash ...

'Oh, *liebling, liebling*,' moaned Uncle Otto. As if he was clutching to his bosom some tiny pet that had been killed in a road accident. I gave him a furtive look, and there was a tear trickling down his leathery pock-marked cheek. Then he said hoarsely, 'Let us go home, Marjorie.'

As we drove back, I looked at Denswick Park with new eyes; Uncle Otto's eyes. Denswick Park had seemed OK till then. It's new, but the people who live there are very keen gardeners, and the builders left a lot of the old oak and beech trees. And nobody I know goes in for garden gnomes. But there are a lot of plastic classical urns full of geraniums; and a few concrete bird-baths and sundials, and plenty of hanging baskets and Fiat Pandas and Vauxhall Cavaliers.

Uncle Otto kept muttering, 'Assassins! Assassins!'

I saw what he meant the following day. He came home with a mass of photocopied plans and drawings. The park had once been laid out by no less than Humphrey Repton himself. With a Chinese lake-garden and temple of 1798. And an orangerie, based on a triumphal arch, by Robert Adam. Uncle Otto stuck the photocopies all over the walls of his bedroom, like pin-ups, and lectured Mum and me till our heads reeled with gazebos and ha-has, Gothic follies and beech avenues. But he made the whole place come alive for us. The de Lane family, who owned it; all the tiny little figures in the drawings, strutting about in wigs and crinolines and three-cornered hats.

The county planning officer rang up, a bit shaky, to ask if his staff had given Otto all the help he needed. Otto called *him* an assassin in his turn. A vandal. The anti-Christ. Mum kept

offering Uncle Otto cups of tea to try to calm him down.
Which he took one sip of, and left lying all over the house.

He went to bed, but I don't think he slept. I heard the
bedsprings twanging under his massive frame all night. Mum
was quite glad to get him out of the house to the Fitzwilliam
the following morning.

Then she went to work; and I settled on the lawn in the
sun, to pretend to swot for my coming history O level. Only
this noise kept echoing through the gardens. It sounded like
some big bird. But its call was so cold, so gloomy, so ominous.
I'd never heard anything as cold and lonely; especially when
the sun kept going behind a cloud.

Then Tom Morland comes belting up our drive. Early-
retired, fit as a fiddle, and our Homewatch co-ordinator. From
the look on his face, I thought Al Capone and Bonnie and
Clyde had just driven up in their bullet-proof Cadillacs.

'Have you seen a peacock in your garden?' he shouts. I turn
over and look, just in time to see this large blur of bright blue,
much bigger than a hen, half fly and half leap through a gap
in the laburnum trees behind the shed where Mum keeps her
lawn-mower.

'There it goes,' Tom shouts, and suddenly our garden and
the one next door are full of Tom's deputy-sheriffs, hot for the
chase. There's a lot of early-retired people live in Denswick
Park. And what with their non-stop lawn-mowing, digging,
hedge-clipping and mulching, with the occasional round of golf
thrown in for relaxation, they're fitter than me, and I play for
the second XV.

Anyway, we had quite an afternoon of it. Tom kept on
asking whether he could use our phone, as he lived at the
other end of the estate. Our very own policeman, Inspector
Blacow, roused from his attempt to sleep off his night-shift,
joined in. There were three Police Pandas (Pandas are very
attentive to Denswick Park). And hordes of these fit brown
pensioners, a big enough Dad's Army to have frightened off
Hitler.

But they seemed totally unable to catch the damned thing.

The shapes of the gardens were against them, you see. We don't have the usual neat rectangular gardens, with fence and privet. Nothing so bourgeois. No, everyone's garden is an odd wavering shape, like a forest glade. And all that's between them are these thick bands of low ornamental trees. It's like a well-weeded jungle. And the peacock kept flying through and over the trees, whereas the pursuers, with English politeness, couldn't break through after it, but had to go and ask permission at the next house ... In the end, even Dad's Army gave up exhausted, and gathered about thirty-strong on our lawn. Tom told them he'd rung every stately home for twenty miles around, and none of them was short of a peacock. (God help Mum's phone-bill!) People wondered what peacocks ate, and whether it would starve to death or die of the bitter cold of an English June. And all the time the damned bird was mocking them with that cold, dreary, ominous ghostly cry, as the sky darkened, and the storm-clouds gathered. Then people began wondering if there was more than one of them; because the calls were sounding from more than one spot in the jungly gardens. But Tom reckoned it was only back-echoes off the houses.

They all went home to have hot baths. Leaving the gardens to the peacock. Or peacocks. Honestly, the racket they made was awful. Made you feel you were living in an enemy-occupied territory. That night we had not only Uncle Otto's bedsprings, but also those awful cries.

I didn't get to sleep till after midnight. And the cries woke me up at four. It was still dark. I opened my dormer window and peered out over the garden-jungle. And it seemed that, incredibly, Tom's lot had risen from their disturbed slumbers and were out in the dark among the ornamental bushes, searching for the peacocks *again*. I couldn't see at all well. But there was the crackle of vegetation underfoot, the sound of bushes being parted, girls giggling and men shouting, and the odd glint or flare of lights. Incredibly, they actually seemed to be *enjoying* it. Even more incredibly, they actually sounded a bit drunk, or at least merry. And some crazy idiot seemed to be carrying a transistor radio playing something classical, like Bach or Vivaldi. I ask you, a ghetto-blaster in Denswick Park at four o'clock in the morning.

There were house-lights coming on, all over the place. Then the noise of an approaching Panda. Several approaching Pandas. I put on my dressing-gown over my pyjamas, and went down into the road to see the fun. All the neighbours were gathering round the Pandas, looking sleepy and bewildered.

Suddenly the thought struck me. If all the neighbours were in the street, who the hell was still crashing and giggling with the ghetto-blaster through our jungly back gardens? Yobs from the town, on a peacock-hunt?

As if they'd heard what I was thinking, it all suddenly stopped. Like a radio being switched off. Silence. Darkness. Peace. Except for the cries of the peacocks, and the solitary slop of a pair of bedroom slippers. We all jumped. The police prepared to move in ...

But it was only Uncle Otto, resplendent in a maroon silk dressing-gown with Chinese dragons embroidered all over it. Without his hornrims, he looked shy, bewildered and vulnerable.

'Vot iss happening? I voss asleep!' Funny how his accent got stronger, when he was half asleep.

Well, there was nothing to do but go back to bed. And lie and listen to the damned peacocks.

The following morning, Denswick Park came as near to a riot as it ever would in its history. I mean, they're friendly people; good neighbours. They feed each other's pets, when they go away on holiday. If a guy's lawn-mower breaks down on a Sunday morning, there's a crowd of five round him to help before you can say 'blown fuse'. But they are *passionate* gardeners. And in the bright morning light, the gardens were a *wreck*. Herbaceous borders trampled flat. Wistarias mauled to pieces. Well-developed geraniums snapped into twenty cuttings for next year. Footprints everywhere in the wet earth.

At first, people blamed Tom Morland and his deputies. But Tom said quite rightly that there'd been no serious damage by dusk the previous night; and none of his people would admit to blundering around in the dark.

And the footprints were all wrong. They weren't Denswick Park footprints. They weren't the green wellies of the elderly, or the trainers of the young. They were square-toed footprints, with high heels. Inspector Blacow said they were punk footprints, yob-from-the-town footprints. And that seemed to satisfy the oldies. (The young had other worries besides herbaceous borders, like O levels, or getting kids to school.) And so an uneasy peace descended; full of the planting of new cuttings, the tying-up of fallen bushes, hoeing and raking. By night, the gardens of Denswick Park would be healed, or at least convalescent ...

But I wasn't so sure. I hadn't seen any yobs in square-toed high-heeled shoes recently. And among the footprints I found a tiny white handkerchief of very fine material, with a beautiful lace edge. Not a yob hanky ...

When Uncle Otto saw it, he frowned, picked it up. His large nose twitched from side to side with passionate sniffing.

'Musk,' he announced. 'The eternal scent of passion. May I borrow this?'

I didn't see why not. I just didn't think it suited him, that's all.

When I got back from my afternoon history O level, feeling like a wrung-out dishcloth, I saw Mum's car in the drive, and the taxi from Cambridge just driving away after dumping Uncle Otto. (He always took taxis; he got lost in buses; he once ended up in Banbury, not knowing where he was, but with a newly evolved theory in his head that eventually became his famous book *The Fall of Sir John Vanbrugh*.) So I knew they were both home.

And they were both standing at the top end of our back garden, staring at an object that had not been there when I left that morning.

A statue, nearly life-size. On a pedestal. A nude female with hollow, drilled blank eyes, and a plentiful supply of hair, arranged to cover up most strategic points, while her carefully disposed hands masked the rest.

I thought they both looked a bit blank, a bit shocked. But they were working very hard, making polite noises.

'Very beautiful. Most carefully placed. Admirable,' said Uncle Otto.

'Yes, it really does something for the garden,' said Mum, doubtfully.

'I do compliment you on your taste,' says Uncle Otto.

'You're much too generous, Otto,' said Mum.

'Not at all. You are a lady of such sensitive taste,' said Otto.

We went indoors to have tea. I suppose that I, like Mum, thought that Otto had bought it for her, as a present for us putting him up for a fortnight. I mean, Otto's frightfully well-off and generous. After that camera he bought me, I'd believe anything of him. And Mum *had* been upset about the damage to her beloved garden. And I think Otto's a bit sweet on her, and he hasn't got a lot of people to spend his money on ...

So it was decidedly odd that as he and I were going to bed, he stopped me on the landing, shuffled and said, 'Erm, erm, have you any idea where your mother ... bought that statue, young Simon? It is so fine ... Georgian ... I should like to have one like it for my little basement patio at home ...'

I looked at him, blankly. Then I thought he was making one of his ponderous Germanic jokes. His dark eyes swam behind his hornrims, unfathomable. So I just shrugged and grinned feebly, and said goodnight. And lay awake a long time, wondering: if Mum hadn't put it there, and Uncle Otto hadn't, just who on earth had? The noise of the peacocks didn't help me get to sleep, either.

I had to get away to school early the following morning, for a French O level. Then I had Physics in the afternoon. So I missed most of the fuss. There were only two police cars left in our road by the time I got home, and they belonged to the regional Fine Art Squad. But I was questioned in my turn. Though why some gang of crooks should have looted all the statuary from the gardens of some unknown stately home, only to dump it in the gardens of Denswick Park overnight ... and all without anybody hearing a thing except peacocks. Bert Alford had a superb sundial, right in the middle of his bed of white alyssum and lobelia. On top of most of the lobelia. Not being a lover of antiques, he was still nearly weeping about the lobelia, and insisting on the police taking the great nasty thing away. The police refused. They had no evidence yet that the thing had been stolen; nobody had reported the theft. They hadn't got a crane, either. The thing must have weighed half a ton.

Mary Webster was in an even worse state. A green, very old bronze derived from Donatello's 'David'. Over life-size. Without even the benefit of a fig-leaf. Where her alpine rockery had been ... Ken and Shirley McCrae had the Three Graces, totally covering their goldfish pond. They were trying to dig in at the side and rescue the goldfish. But the weirdest thing was that somebody had cut a path straight across the turf of Bill Williams' lawn; exposing fine yellow gravel underneath that Bill had never guessed was there. The path stopped at his hedge, but continued next door through Dougie Morton's rubbish heap and on to Maureen Harvester's vegetable patch. It stopped when it reached Bert Alford's sundial ...

The police announced themselves baffled, and drove away.

Uncle Otto inspected every item and pronounced it superb Georgian, with great arm-waving enthusiasm. Mum had to get him away from the neighbours quick, before they lynched him.

He said sadly afterwards, over an undrunk cup of tea, 'Such strange people, the English. Such love of little plants, and yet they hate great beauty in stone ...'

Mum spent about two hours cooking supper. People kept ringing her up to complain about yet another atrocity. The peacocks were worse than ever. There seemed to be about six of them now, calling to each other as night fell, across the darkened gardens. I felt in a total frazzle. I just knew I was going to fail Geography tomorrow: I couldn't swot at all; my head was buzzing, like there was some great thunderstorm brewing.

Then the noises started from the gardens; crashing and laughter. A rather nasty, giggly, *sexy* sort of laughter. I've never *heard* an orgy, being only fifteen, but it's how I would imagine an orgy sounds.

I looked out of my dormer-bedroom window, where I'd gone to swot. And I could have sworn there was somebody moving at the bottom of our garden, between the shed and the magnolias.

I sneaked downstairs. Mum was on the blower, trying to ring somebody up, but complaining she was just getting a funny buzz, instead of the dialling tone. Uncle Otto was sitting slumped in a chair, looking as if it was all beyond him, holding the little lace handkerchief I'd given him in his big hands and staring at it.

I sneaked out of the back door. Yes, there was something moving behind the shed. Something that glittered golden, in the faint light coming from our bungalow windows. The way it moved made me think it was a girl, somehow. I suddenly thought that if I caught her, the whole mystery might be solved ... I ran like mad. And suddenly she was running in front of me. Up a narrow alleyway between high hedges, that I hadn't realized was there. Must be in *somebody's* garden ...

She was laughing as she ran. An excited, breathless laughing. And she wasn't running very fast, because she was wearing a long dress she had to hold up with both hands, to avoid tripping up. And she kept half looking back over her shoulder, as if she *wanted* me to catch her.

And then she gave up; stopped and faced me. She had one hand against her heaving side, and one ...

Against the sundial I'd seen earlier in Bert Alford's garden.

How could I see her so clearly in the dark? I paused, suddenly wary, with the hair actually lifting on the back of my neck.

Then I realized I could see her because there were huge paper lanterns hung in the branches of the trees overhead. Paper lanterns with real candles flickering inside them. Chinese lanterns. Was Bert Alford mad? I mean, it was June; not Christmas or anything. But the girl was in fancy dress ... her hair, piled in a great beehive on her head, was snow-white. Was she really a girl, or an old woman? I couldn't see her eyes; there was a black mask over them, like one of those masks highwaymen wore, in the stupid old movies. There were black spots on her rounded cheeks. And her golden dress was low-cut almost to the waist, and her heaving boobs were nearly dropping out. And her little teeth showed in a wicked, suggestive grin.

And suddenly I didn't want to go any nearer. In fact I wanted to run like hell. But I was rooted to the spot.

Slowly, daintily, suggestively, she minced up towards me. Put her little hands up to my face. Smiled.

Her teeth were *black*. Her breath was a mixture of sweetness and decay. And the smell of her ... sweat, and not tonight's sweat, either. Old stale sweat. *Yuk*.

Too late I heard footsteps behind me, and tried to turn. Something smashed down on my head, and everything went confused.

I came to being bundled along, with my arms twisted up behind my back. All I could see, looking behind me, were the feet and legs of the guys who were frog-marching me. Black highly polished shoes with square toes and highish heels and steel buckles (though the shoes were a bit wet and the steel buckles starting to rust). The legs were massive and muscular in white cotton stockings; the cotton wrinkling as they walked. They didn't look like girls' feet and legs. But then it wasn't girlish hands that were twisting the life out of me. What kind of crazy new punkish fashion was this?

'Let me go, you yobs,' I shouted.

They twisted my arms harder and hurried me all the faster. Then, as we came out of the trees and bushes, they stopped to draw breath and let me stand upright. I gasped. Before me stood a great house, with pediment and portico, and every window lit with a softer glow than electric light. And on its terrace, and on the sloping grass below, walked people in fantastic costume. The men in breeches and white stockings, and skirted coats stiff with gold brocade, that glinted in the dim light from the windows. The women in long dresses that spread out stiffly from their waists. But they all had that shocking white hair, and all wore masks. They paraded, they preened, they greeted each other and walked arm in arm. Some of the women had spectacles on a long stick, which they held up to peer at anything that interested them.

There were wilder things going on in the bushes behind. Chasing and wild gleeful screaming, and some grunting sounds I wouldn't want to go into. I thought I had found my orgy.

But again they thrust my head down and urged me on. And as they did, I realized why the whole weird scene looked so oddly familiar. It was an exact copy of Uncle Otto's photocopied views of the old Denswick Park. Even to all the carefully drawn figures of the little people.

I thought I must be caught up in some fantastic nightmare; only the pain in my head and back and arms seemed far too real ...

I was bundled up a long flight of stone steps. Through doors. The faint music like Bach or Vivaldi became really loud. I could see the disciplined feet of dancers, tapping, kicking, pirouetting. Then the music died, and all the feet stopped, and I knew that they were all regarding me with censorious horror, as I was bundled across the huge black-and-white squares of the marble floor.

I was thrust into another room. A darker candle-lit room, full of large male legs and a smell of animal sweat and booze and urine. There was a huge dark sideboard, doors wide open, full of chamber-pots, and some of them weren't empty, either. As I looked, some large male hand reached out one of the pots, and I heard the sound of somebody using it, right there in public. God, the stench; I shall never forget the stench as long as I live.

And then they let me stand upright. And all the faces were glaring at me red-cheeked, thick-lipped, drunken, sweating. And entirely hating. As if I had no right to exist; worse, as if I was some obscene blot on the landscape. One seemed to be the boss; a bull of a man, with huge chest and broad shoulders, smoothly encased in red cloth, with brass epaulettes. He shouted something to the men holding me, and they answered with trembling respect. The language was funny; almost like English, and yet not quite, twisted somehow, so you couldn't quite get what they were saying, though I caught two words.

'Trespasser' and 'poacher'.

The bull-like man walked over to me, and shouted something at me I couldn't understand. Next second, he had crashed his fist into my face. I tasted blood in my mouth, and one of my teeth felt loose.

He pulled back his fist to hit me again. He had little mad bright-blue eyes, that looked as if they thought they owned the whole earth ...

But before he could hit me again, there was an interruption. Somebody else was dragged in. Uncle Otto. God, he looked a mess. He'd lost his spectacles in the struggle, and the great dark eyes were peering half blindly everywhere, and his dark hair was standing up in a crest, like he was a frightened parrot. Still, I was very glad to see him. At least it proved this wasn't a nightmare.

Or did it?

Because now a third figure was being frog-marched in, and allowed to stand upright.

Inspector Blacow. In full uniform. They must have caught him about to go on night-shift. He even had his uniform cap in his hand.

Now Inspector Blacow is a fine figure of a man. He's built like a bull as well, and in uniform his collar is whiter than white, and his badges gleam like silver mirrors. And he has more authority than any Chief Constable. Bet he's never had to hit anybody in his whole career; a *look* from Inspector Blacow would have quelled Al Capone.

Now, he broke the lackey's hold on him with one flick of his arms. They knew authority when they saw it; they fell back, cowed. Inspector Blacow slowly straightened his cuffs and put his uniform cap on his head. He said to the bull-like figure in red, 'I'll put you and your kinky mates away for life.'

The bull-like figure in red did flinch for a second, then came back with an even harder glare. I mean, they just stood there and glared at each other. They were so alike; both so absolutely certain of themselves. Of their invincible authority. Like a pair of bulls about to charge each other. And then, they both began frowning, in a puzzled way. The man in red was starting to doubt Inspector Blacow was a mere trespasser; and Inspector Blacow was starting to wonder whether the man in red really was some kind of kink . . .

And in between them, helpless, gawping, half blind, pathetic, was the ridiculous figure of Uncle Otto.

Except that his eyes, even half blind, were still intelligent. And suddenly, I could swear, a sort of understanding of what was happening seemed to dawn on him. He said, in a low voice, *'Mein Gott!'* and clapped his huge hand to his high forehead.

And suddenly I was falling. In darkness. I gave one convulsive kick, then I splashed down into water. I thought I was drowning; clawed out and got a handful of what felt like thick stems. Shot upwards and breathed clear air. Then struggled to my feet. The water was only about four feet deep, but it must have broken my fall.

I opened my eyes, and found I was standing in the ornamental lily pond which is a prime new feature of the Denswick Park Social and Sports Club. And, quite near, there were convulsions where first Uncle Otto and then Inspector Blacow heaved to the surface.

'What the . . .?' said Inspector Blacow, fishing for his cap with an instinct born of long experience, and glaring round.

But there was nothing to see. Except the Sports and Social Club, and the back gardens and little hipped bungalow roofs of the Denswick Park Estate. And the little knots of residents who slowly gathered round the pool, to complain to him that the yobs had been vandalizing their gardens again, and one of them must have had a ghetto-blaster playing Vivaldi ...

Inspector Blacow kept his head; I'll say that for him. Crimes might have been committed, but public belief in the sanity of the police force must be the first priority.

'We chased them,' he said. 'They threw us in here. They made off in that direction.' He pointed vaguely towards the next suburb. Then he added, consulting his watch (which was waterproof and still going) by the light of one of their torches, 'I have to be on duty in five minutes; I'll send somebody to take your evidence in the morning.'

Well, he certainly took *my* evidence, though I don't think it ever appeared in any police report. I told him everything but one fact; that look of dawning comprehension that had come on to Uncle Otto's face, the moment before he clapped his hand to his forehead and we all fell down into the goldfish pond.

Inspector Blacow wiped his sweating forehead with a spotless white handkerchief and said, 'Thanks. It's nice to know I'm not going stark-staring bonkers. Or at least I'm not the only one. What do you think really happened?'

'Some sort of time-slip,' I said. 'We must have slipped back two hundred years. To the time when the real Denswick Park was first built. I've seen pictures of it. And those people. And their clothes.' I took him and showed him the photocopies, still pinned to the walls of Uncle Otto's newly vacated bedroom. He agreed with me, pulling his lip thoughtfully.

Then he said, 'That room where we saw that bloke in red ... where's that on the plan?'

I pointed it out.

'It was on the first floor,' he said. 'The demolished first floor. Just above where the new goldfish pond is now. So when the time-slip finished, we fell fifteen feet into the pond. It saved our necks.'

No fool, our Inspector Blacow.

He added, 'All those statues and things have gone too. The Superintendent is going mad, wondering what to put in his report to the Chief Constable.'

'Perhaps they were part of the time-slip?' I suggested, as calmly as I could.

'Yeah.' Then he added, 'I'd have liked to have talked to your Uncle Otto.'

'He's gone,' I said. 'First train this morning. He had an urgent appointment. In Vienna. Mum drove him to the station.'

'He must be a very interesting bloke. I'd like to have known what he thought of it . . .'

Wouldn't we all? But all Uncle Otto had said, when I shook hands with him, and wished him goodbye, was, 'Perhaps I love the old times too much. They are pleasant to read about, but not, perhaps, to live in. The Age of Reason was not perhaps so reasonable. Perhaps even' – he looked sadly at all the well-mown lawns – 'this is more peaceful: to grow flowers and get on with your neighbours, and to harm no one.'

I suppose that's the best testimonial the Denswick Park Estate will ever get.

Warren, Sharon
and Darren

1

Sharon met Warren when she was between job-creation schemes, on a morning her Giro cheque hadn't come. She had a row with her mother about money, and walked out in a huff, without having any breakfast.

By the time she got to the town centre, she wished she hadn't. It was a hot muggy morning in May, her head felt stuffed with cotton wool, and she felt sick. And it was far too early. None of her gang would be at the seats in the town square till after lunch; she'd only got up early herself because of the Giro cheque. The town was full of people in work, spending money.

She went round staring in the shop windows. But she'd stared into them all the day before, and there was nothing new. The cake shops were the worst; fat middle-aged women in the cafés, stuffing their faces with cream doughnuts. Her own stomach was churning like a cement-mixer, and she had four pence in her purse. Even the public library had no charms. She walked and walked, and soon she was just walking in circles, and the circles got dizzier and dizzier. What was the point of it all? Two months before she had any hope of getting on another job-creation scheme, and that would be rubbish. The last boss had been kind; but once he'd found her voice wasn't posh enough to answer the phone, he'd just had her clearing out cardboard boxes full of old wire coat-hangers, then making the tea, then polishing brass handles and making more tea, cleaning already-clean windows. For the last month, his ingenuity at finding her jobs exhausted, he'd suggested she bring a book to read . . .

She was walking blindly now; her legs felt like rubber tubes; it was suddenly getting awfully dark . . .

Then a hand grabbed her arm; a hand like a steel vice. She looked up, startled, to see a large bony muscular face staring down at her, two-thirds shining bald head, and the most incredible purple Mohican haircut she'd ever seen.

She honestly thought her last moment had come. She'd wandered into the wrong part of the shopping precinct; there were dozens of the Mohican lot, lounging against the railings of the pedestrian overpass, looking at her in that grinning sort of way. And those hard-faced girls with the short bleached hair . . .

She looked wildly back to the one who had hold of her; she opened her mouth to scream. Then she noticed the eyes in that lean face.

They were bright blue. And they were *kind*.

The mouth opened.

'You all right, love?' he asked.

'I'm just thirsty,' she said. It was all she could think of to say. Then she blushed; 'cos it sounded like she was cadging.

'Wotcher want? A lager?'

'A glass of water would do.'

'Getcher a still-orange. Sit down afore you fall down.' He dumped her with painful force, in one of those wood and concrete benches. Shouted, 'An leave her alone, you *******,' to his mates, and departed.

He obviously was some sort of boss. They left her alone; though the bleach-haired girls muttered spitefully among themselves. Then he was back with a still-orange from a kiosk. He must have run; he'd spilled so much the outside of the glass was first slippery, and then sticky. She drank it gratefully.

He told him his name was Warren.

She told him her name was Sharon.

And that was the start of it.

*

It should never have got off the ground. He wasn't her sort; and she wasn't his. If her mother ever found out she'd even been seen walking around with him, World War III would have started. Her Dad might be on the dole at the moment, but the Robinsons were respectable. They might live in a council house; but they had the best front garden on the estate. And her Dad had an allotment, and grew all his own vegetables and even kept hens for eggs.

Warren lived at the other end of the estate; his front garden was full of bits of rusting motorbikes. He had a brother in the nick for stealing and crashing a car. And his Mohican mates had no more time for her than her friends had for him.

Romeo and Juliet didn't have it any rougher.

But she couldn't resist the kindness of his eyes. And in his eyes, she was a proper lady, a little princess.

So they became outcasts from their tribes. But it was summer, and they were in love, and the countryside wasn't far away.

So they walked. Like all the walking dolies, they were very fit. Thirty miles a day was nothing for them. They walked in the fields and they walked in the woods; though they had to keep a wary eye open for farmers. Farmers might have let her get away with trespassing, for she was little and pretty in her faded jeans and best floppy sweater that her Mum had knitted. But one glimpse of Warren's hair and they became homicidal shotgun-flourishing dog-loosing maniacs.

Sometimes they tried a country pub, when Warren had money. Warren's money was funny. All her own friends had the same pattern. A bit to spend when the Giro came through, and slowly down to dead skint by the end of the week. Warren was dead broke some weeks, so she had to buy him a packet of fags, each one of which he lit up three times, getting smaller and smaller. Other weeks, he had such a wad of blue-backs in his pocket it scared her. She never dared ask where he got it; it was summer and a dream. To ask would shatter the dream . . .

Anyway, the pubs weren't a success. The moment the landlords laid eyes on Warren, they got into a pale sweaty panic and rang for the police, even when he'd paid for the drinks . . . Sharon often dreamed of a Warren with a crew-cut of normal colour, and nice jeans and a white sweat-shirt, instead of his sweaty black sleeveless one. But she never dared say anything. He had his pride; she dared not shatter the dream.

But she taught him about cows; how to tell a Friesian from a Jersey; and about sheep and lambs, and the names of flowers. And when they made love in some cool wood (not all the way) his hands were as gentle as his eyes.

Sometimes they would borrow his brother's old banger. But only in the dusk, because Warren didn't have a licence, and the car wouldn't pass its MOT. And Warren drove slowly and carefully, not to catch the eye of any Panda.

It was on one such evening, warm and dusky blue, that the odd thing happened. They were snuggled up in a wood that reeked of wild garlic. The white flowers were shining all around them. Warren had just said they smelt like onions, and she'd told him what they were, and he'd said they were safe from Dracula, anyway, when all the air outside the wood began to shine with a strange pale light. The branches of the trees stood out against it like black lace. They lay, paralysed, trying to make out what it could *be*. It was much too bright for the moon. Warren thought it might be the fuzz, but there was no sound of fuzz beetlecrushers trampling down the undergrowth. There was a sort of tinkling music.

Sharon kept on thinking of an open-air production of *A Midsummer Night's Dream* her class had been dragged to for GCE in the fifth year. Being in the open air, you couldn't hear half of what the actors were saying; and the other half she couldn't understand anyway; but she'd liked the music, and it had been a bit like this music. Mixed up with something by Mike Oldfield.

The music went on and on; the light got brighter and brighter. It made her realize how tiny the wood was they were lying in; no bigger than a pocket-handkerchief, really. The light reached down through the branches, so she could see every flower and blade of grass, and every wrinkle in Warren's boots.

'They're after *us*,' muttered Warren. 'Nobody else here, is there?' He wrapped himself round her protectively, till she felt buried inside a warm panting mountain of him. She could tell he would have sold his life dearly, defending her; but there was nothing to defend her against . . .

She thought she fainted; certainly there was a sense of waking up afterwards, with Warren still wrapped tightly round her, snoring his head off. She poked him. 'It's gone. The light an' the music . . .'

He came awake with a snort and a grunt. They lay a long time, but nothing else happened, and in the end they went thoughtfully home.

'Mebbe it was a flying saucer,' said Warren, as he dropped her a hundred yards from her gate. But she could tell he was glad it hadn't been the fuzz, on account of his brother's car.

Two months later, she became convinced she was pregnant. She woke early and lay in bed feeling both sick and terrified. Mainly at the thought of telling anybody.

But in the end, choosing another good snuggled-up time in a wood, she told Warren.

'You musta gone too far, Warren,' she said, ever so gently. This was the point where the fellers always walked out on you . . .

'I didn't go too far, *honest*.' His kind blue eyes were wide and worried, but also quite baffled. 'I *know* I didn't go too far.' But he didn't back away, like she was frightened he would; he just hugged her tighter. Like she was the crown jewels.

Not like her parents. She was getting ready one night to go out. Mum had just ironed her best jeans, and gave them to her, hot off the ironing-board, to put on.

And there, right in front of them, she couldn't do the top button up. And as she struggled, breaking out in a sweat and getting red in the face, Mum guessed.

Her parents sat with faces of stone.

'Who is it? Who's the lad?' said Dad. She knew it could still have been all right. If the lad had been some college student, or some apprentice with good prospects . . .

But when she said, 'Warren Slingsby,' and Mum said, 'Oh, God, not *the* Slingsbys,' and an Arctic silence descended on that cosy little room with the flying ducks on the wall, where she'd lived since she was two, she knew there was nothing left to do but pack her bag and go. They were still sitting there in their armchairs, like statues, when she looked round the door to say goodbye.

They didn't even ask her where she was going; she supposed they knew there was only one place she could go.

But as she walked through the estate, from her end to his, head up, blushing, imagining the whole estate was watching her downfall, she had the oddest feeling. A feeling that someone was with her, who was going to look after her. Not just Warren, bless him, though he would do his best. But somebody wise and strong, who knew exactly what he was doing and was a hundred per cent on her side. She wondered if it could be God; in a wild sort of way. But she'd gone to the chapel with her parents all her life; more than long enough to know God wouldn't look after her sort. She wondered if she was going mad. But she felt too looked-after and warm and cosy to be going mad.

She needed all that warmth and cosiness when she got to Warren's. It wasn't that they *condemned* her; they just weren't interested. Half the Slingsby clan had been born out of wedlock. The lads, who were lounging about the room sipping cans of lager, kicking oily spare-parts of motorbike idly about the stained carpet with their boots, went straight back to an argument about the World Cup. The women shrugged sympathetically but briefly, and went back to their squabbles about the stinginess of the fellers. The women made a lot of loud and bitter noise; but you could tell they didn't have much pull. For that matter, there was so much coming and going of males and females through the ever-open front door that you couldn't tell who exactly were Slingsbys and who were not. There were kids everywhere, demanding grub and sweets in monotonous whines, and getting the occasional thump for their pains. The whole thing was about as welcoming as Euston Station in the rush-hour . . .

Warren sat in the corner of one of the settees, cuddling her and telling her it would be OK, in between joining in the argument about the World Cup. They spent the night in a sleeping-bag on the floor of the lounge, which they shared with two other couples in a more joyously festive mood than themselves . . . Sharon had never known such outward desolation. Yet this friend in her head kept telling her it would be all right . . .

And amazingly, by the next night it was.

A caravan. A huge but ramshackle caravan. Parked in a farmyard just on the edge of town. OK, the fields of the farm were now under a new council estate. And the farmhouse was inhabited by blokes who came and went in flash cars late at night, and you *never* asked what they did, apart from being mates of Warren's. But the caravan stood in a little field of dirty grass, and there was a clothes-line; and a wood at the back, even though it had lost a lot of branches to the climbing, feuding kids of the new estate.

They had their own front door, three miles from the Slingsby clan. And a pile of blankets and a mattress. And another mate of Warren's was coming tomorrow to wire up the lights and cooker.

She told Warren he was the most wonderful bloke in the world.

Warren shook his head, baffled. 'Weren't me. Bloke I know just walked up to me in t'Mosley Arms an' said did I know anybody who wanted a caravan for fifty quid. It all just *happened*.'

Four months later, Sharon was rushed into hospital, late one night. It was all over amazingly quickly. But Sharon just lay in a daze.

The baby weighed seven whole pounds; there was nothing

in the least *premature* about him, sister insisted. A lovely boy; a *beautiful* boy. Sharon tried to tell her that nine months ago, she hadn't even known Warren; hadn't done more than kissed a boy at a party.

Sister told her not to be silly; and through the open door of her office Sharon heard her raging to Staff Nurse about the ignorance and fecklessness of these young things.

But everyone adored the child. His eyes were a beautiful blue; everyone said just like Warren's. But they weren't like Warren's at all. Warren's eyes were dark blue, and warm. The child's were a pale blue, and *cool*. But he was round and rosy from the start, with ash-blond hair. And every moment of the day, there was some female bending over him, adoring him. Even the Robinsons were won round enough to cash-in some premium-bonds, and buy him a decent pram. And more than ever, Sharon calmly felt that somebody big and powerful was on her side . . .

There was the matter of the kids from the estate, for instance. They haunted the wood behind the caravan at the weekends, tearing down the trees, and even throwing clods of earth at any washing Sharon dared put out, the week she returned home from hospital.

One day, in despair, she rushed out to have it out with them. She immediately wished she hadn't. There were about fifteen of them, with more gathering every minute. They began throwing clods not only at the washing, but at the van itself. Then at Sharon . . .

She dissolved into tears.

And then the clods stopped flying. She looked up. The whole mob of kids was standing stock-still; frozen. With very startled looks on their faces. As if there was something terrifying standing behind Sharon. She turned round, expecting to see Warren. But there was nobody.

Next second there was a scuffling behind her, and she turned again to see every kid from the estate in full flight, as fast as their legs could carry them.

They never bothered her again; they never even came into the wood any more. Peace descended.

But it was the matter of the apples that really frightened her. She'd been pushing the baby round the local market in his bright new pram. She'd come to the end of her shopping when she saw the lovely red apples. She adored apples, red apples; the sort you could polish with a cloth until they shone like glass. But the apples, even in the market, were thirty pence a pound, and when she looked in her purse, she only had twenty-five pence left. So she trudged wearily home, apple-less.

Or so she thought, until she came to unpack the shopping. On the top was a bag of red apples. And underneath was another pound. And another. And all already polished till they shone like glass . . .

She looked at the baby, still in his pram. The baby smiled at her, with his cool blue eyes. Only that was daft; Mum said babies couldn't smile until they were three months old; before that, it was just them bringing up wind.

They called the baby Darren. Everybody thought that was a marvellous joke; Warren, Sharon and Darren. But the Methodist waxed strong in Sharon. She would like the baby baptized properly; but the Methodists wouldn't baptize a baby when the parents weren't married, she was sure of that. And the Slingsbys were as fervently against marriage and baptism as the Methodists were for it. And she could never bear to walk up the aisle of that Methodist church with Warren in a purple Mohican haircut; after all, her parents had told the other Methodists that she was just working away from home as a nanny. (Hence the gift of the posh pram.) Oh, her world was in *such* a mess. She lapsed into a daydream. Warren minus the Mohican, in a nice suit and open-necked shirt (even she would not go as far as giving him a *tie*; even daydreams have their limits) walking with her up the aisle . . .

Being a sensible girl, she came out of the daydream after half an hour, and got on with peeling the potatoes for chips for tea.

Half an hour later, Warren walked in. Wearing a nice suit, and an open-necked shirt; bald as a coot, where the Mohican had been. Saying, 'I think we should get married, love. We can't live like pigs all our lives.'

Speechless and terrified, she gave him his tea. He seemed quite unaware of any change in himself. He didn't even tell her he'd got the suit and shirt from a mate. He didn't even keep feeling his bald scalp every two minutes, like Mohicans always did for a month after getting rid of it . . . he just carried on as if he'd never been any different.

She went on being terrified; there *was* a big friend who was on her side; who would give her anything she wished. And she was quite sure it wasn't God. God did miracles, maybe. But not miracles involving shirts and suits. God wouldn't be so frivolous. And God wouldn't take Warren's Mohican off him, and even the *memory* of his Mohican. God wouldn't make Warren into her *puppet* to dress and undress like a doll.

She wished there was somebody she could ask. But there was no one else; just the baby. She looked at Darren. He was watching her, with that cool smile again. She leapt to her feet, and tried to burp him for wind.

There wasn't any wind. There never was any wind with Darren. Like there were no outbursts of crying, or waking in the night. Darren was a perfect baby in every respect.

Darren continued to smile at her.

That night, she *prayed* to her unknown big friend that Warren should be given back his Mohican and his old sleeveless black sweat-shirt; that he should be himself again. She prayed half the night, restless in Warren's innocent arms, so he several times stirred restlessly and said,

'What's the matter, love?'

But her big friend didn't listen. In the morning, Warren was still bald, with just a haze of fuzz over his whole shining scalp, where hair was starting to grow. He put on his new shirt and his new suit, before he went off for the day . . .

She swore she would never wish for anything else again.

But that night, he came home and threw a wad of blue-backs into her lap so big it terrified her. Nearly a thousand pounds.

'We'll need that, love,' he said. 'We're gonna get married. Gonna get young Darren baptized proper-like. And to hell wi' what me family say.'

She stared at the money in her lap as if it was some cobra, swaying its hooded head before a poisoned strike. There was no way Warren could've made that money honestly. She had visions of the fuzz coming up to the caravan door, to take him away for years and years. And it would be her fault for wishing to get married. Her ghastly Methodist fault.

She prayed he wouldn't be caught this time. She prayed he would stop doing this kind of thing, which would mean the nick for him, sooner or later.

For some reason, she looked across at the baby in his carrycot.

He was smiling up at her again.

Some nights later, Warren came home carrying a briefcase and wearing a tie; a very quiet dark red tie with thin blue and white stripes, that her father would certainly have approved of. The fuzz on his head was denser now; in a few days it would be a respectable crew-cut. Warren, she thought desperately, Warren, where are you?

Out loud, with a voice in which she could hardly suppress the trembling, she said,

'What's the briefcase for, love?'

'Harry Traub – old mate of mine – get me on selling insurance. I got the knack, Sharon. I seem to know – just where to call at, what to say to them – money for old rope.'

But the roughness seemed to have gone out of his voice. He spoke as posh as she did, now. Though that wasn't very posh. Oh, Warren, Warren, where *are* you?

2

By the time the District Nurse caught up with Sharon and Darren, it was spring. The wood behind the caravan, unvandalized all winter, was lovely with the smells of bud and blossom and bluebells. Warren had painted the van, inside and out, on Sundays, which was the only spare time he now had from the insurance business.

But the District Nurse still did not approve of babies being brought up in vans, however cheerfully painted; her nose wrinkled.

Sharon's heart sank. The nurse was the worst sort. The brisk but-surely sort, who asked questions and didn't listen to your answers. The sort who talked over her shoulder while she poked in your cupboards without as much as a by-your-leave.

Darren was walking by the time she came; and saying things like, 'Warren gone in car-car.' He followed the nurse about, giving her hard stares.

Finally, the woman settled on the fitted cupboard-seat, and consulted the official notes from her briefcase.

'Let's see ... the little chap was born in ... December. December ... the ... third.' She looked at Darren, who had lifted down the biscuit-tin and handed it to Sharon, hinting it was time for elevenses. 'That ... makes ... him ... just six months ... old.' Her eyes, from being as wide as saucers, settled into narrow slits, like a bird of prey seeing its new victim.

'He's very ... advanced ... for his age,' said Sharon, defensively. She didn't know much about kids, being an only child; but Darren's rapid growth had worried even her.

'That ... is ... no ... six month old,' gritted the nurse. 'That child is at least eighteen months old.' She turned to Sharon in grim righteous fury. 'Who is this child? What have you done with your own baby? This will have to be *reported*.'

A vision of policemen came into Sharon's mind; of courts and grim-faced women who would take Darren away from her, and put him into care. Who might accuse her of kidnap and murder. She began to cry.

'Mummy *cry*,' said Darren, in a dreadful voice she'd never heard before.

Sharon looked up swiftly through her tears. Darren was standing staring at the nurse. But it was the nurse who looked peculiar. She sat as still as a statue; with her officious biro frozen an inch away from her notebook. Sharon realized she wasn't even *breathing*. Her face was turning purple . . .

'Darren!' she screamed. 'Darren. *Don't*.' It was odd, she thought afterwards, how she never had any doubt it was Darren who was doing it.

Darren gave her a swift, puzzled look. Not unkind; a look that simply wanted her to make her mind up.

'Put the lady down, Darren,' she said, as if the nurse was the tin of biscuits.

Darren must have done. The nurse immediately started breathing again, panting in great lungfulls till her face returned to a healthy pink. When she finally got her breath back she turned to Sharon, smiled apologetically and said, 'Sorry. I went all over swimmy for a moment.' She looked quite friendly and mummish now. '*Anno Domini*, my dear, *anno Domini*. It comes to us all in the end. Do forgive me. Now, let's have a look at this splendid little chap. Hasn't he got *lovely* blue eyes. And that *beautiful* hair – like white silk. You do keep him beautifully . . . I don't think I'll need to call and check up on his progress again.' She even accepted a cup of tea, and took Darren on her lap. He went to her with his most cherubic smile. She left at last, saying she could hardly bear to tear herself away from so lovely a child.

The matter of his age and progress seemed quite wiped from her mind. That scared Sharon as much as the nurse nearly choking to death. Left alone with Darren again, she dared a quick, furtive, guilty look at him. He smiled at her, coolly, reassuringly. As if to say, don't worry little mummy dear! She knew that he loved her, in his cool little way.

And anyway, what had it amounted to? The nurse was old. Perhaps she had had some kind of fit. And in the fright of it, had forgotten all about Darren's age. Or got scared that Sharon might report her funny fit and get her sacked. *That* must be why she'd got friendly and sucked up to Darren. He was only *little*; fancy blaming him for what had happened!

She told Warren the nurse had been, when he got home, but she didn't tell him about the nurse's fit. She didn't want to worry him; he was tired, as usual, after a long successful day selling insurance. He was tired so often now. They didn't make love much any more; and although he played with Darren when Darren was awake, he looked quite glad when Darren was already asleep when he got home. He wasn't so much fun as when he had his Mohican. She wished he didn't have to work so hard.

'Gotta promotion,' said Warren, immediately. So immediately she gaped. 'Harry Traub's makin' me under-manager. I still gotta show the new young blokes how it's done. But I won't be out sellin' so much; put me feet up in the office a bit. How does it feel to be married to a risin' young executive?'

Very shaken, she hugged him and told him he was wonderful.

'Had a good day,' he mumbled into the hair on top of her head. 'Gotta chance of a house, an' all. We can't live like pigs all our life. Old lady Harry sold insurance to has died. Son's out in Saudi for another year . . . doesn't know if he wants to keep the house or not. Wrote to Harry asking him if he could let it fully furnished for a year . . . Harry's got the keys . . .'

The earth seemed to move under her feet. She loved the van, the little field, the wood. 'I've been happy here,' she said stubbornly. '*We've* been happy here . . .'

'I can't bring business mates here, love. Ruin me image . . . I mean, like, what did that nurse think of us bringin' up young Darren in a tip like this?'

She loathed his new business mates, the few she had met. Sharp young thieves in suits with sharp waistcoats. She'd liked the Mohicans better; even Warren's awful family. At least they'd been . . . *honest* crooks. Crooks who didn't swank about Campari and Marbella . . . She stared desperately over Warren's shoulder, wondering how she could persuade him to stay in the caravan.

Darren came out of the door of his little sleeping-compartment. He had his teddy bear trailing from one hand, and a thumb in his mouth. But his eyes, on hers, were cool and smiling.

It'll be all right, dear little mummy dear . . .

And it was. It wasn't a slick glass-wall house, in the middle of a slick glass-wall estate. It was old, but solid, with great big chimneys and bay windows, and a long grassy garden at the back, where the old lady had kept a few hens and a goat. Sharon managed to rescue hens and goat from execution, and soon grew fond of them. Two fat cats turned up, obviously members of the old lady's family who'd been lying low to suss out the next owners. They adored Sharon from the moment she opened the first tin of cat-food she found in the cupboard. There was also a little wood.

Darren smiled at her; you see, I told you it would be all right, dear little mummy dear! Sharon, lying awake in the night, wondered if the old lady would have died when she did, if Darren hadn't wanted her to have the old lady's house . . . But she'd been a very old lady . . . eighty-nine. And she didn't seem to bear any grudge. Her white-haired picture, cuddling her brawny fifty-year-old son, beamed at Sharon from the sitting-room mantelpiece. The whole sunny house welcomed her. There was even a handwritten book of the old lady's recipes, sitting in the kitchen drawer, that Sharon found easy to use.

And oddly. Warren's sharp little business friends, who eyed Sharon's legs and figure, and had been known to pinch her bum when Warren wasn't looking, came once, but never came again. He did business with them over a quick drink after work instead; and still got home by six thirty.

But she used to look at the crewcut young executive sitting opposite her at dinner, and think about the Mohican who first

49

took her out into the woods, and wonder if he minded being Darren's puppet-father. One evening, she fetched her favourite photo of the old Mohican with his mates, a can of lager raised triumphantly in one hand, laughing . . . She showed Warren, shyly, when he asked what she had in her hand.

His nose wrinkled in disgust.

'Didn't you like being like that? Free?' she asked.

'Free to bloody starve? Free to be bored outa me brain? D'you think I *liked* bein' like that? All screwed-up an' hatin' inside? Wantin' to smash things? I swore to kill meself if I reached thirty wi' no job. I wasn't stupid, you know. Even if I made meself look it . . . Don't you think I like havin' money? Goin' into posh restaurants and havin' them call me sir? Oh, Sharon, for God's sake grow up.' He tore up the photo and threw it in the kitchen fire.

Darren was nowhere to be seen . . .

'You never go an' see your family now,' she said.

'That bunch of stupid dead-beats. What did they ever do for me, except pinch the last money outta me jeans, given half a chance . . .'

She cried. He cuddled her, and was the old Warren again, even down to calling her a silly cow, which comforted her strangely.

He wasn't Darren's puppet after all, was he?

Darren proved that, the next autumn. They went for a walk, up on the moors. It was nearly his first birthday. But he was as big as a three year old, running everywhere, and asking endless questions that neither Warren, nor Sharon could answer.

'He oughta be at school,' said Warren.

'For God's sake,' said Sharon, 'he's one year old. The neighbours are startin' to ask questions – saying how big he's growing an' all. We're goin' to have to move again, you know. Soon.' The thought made her deeply depressed. She loved the old lady's house.

'I'd like to live up here,' said Warren, grandly. 'Up on the moors wi' a good view. Like that song, "On a clear day, you can see forever" like. A big house, wi' battlements, like Vicker's Brewery's got. An' a big oak door wi' a big bell-pull. An' all those sticky-out windows . . .'

'They're called bay windows an' . . .' Sharon stopped, and gasped. Over Warren's shoulder, stuck by itself in the middle of the moor all on its own, where no building had been before, where no building could possibly be, was a large house. With battlements like Vicker's Brewery, and bay windows, and a large oak door. From that distance, she could not see if it had a big bell-pull or not.

'An' all new inventions, like solar heating panels on the roof . . .'

Before Sharon's very eyes, silver solar panels grew across the roof.

'An' a wall all round the garden, and big gates like Warrington Town Hall . . .'

Before Sharon's appalled eyes, the garden wall grew, *and* the gates. But inside them remained the gorse and heather of the open hillside.

'An' one of them dishes for satellite TV . . .'

A silver dish grew obligingly, quicker than a speeded-up flower on TV, on the tallest of Vicker's Brewery's battlements.

'An' them white tables wi' umbrellas on the terrace, like they have in pubs. Wi' Carlsberg Lager on them . . .'

Dutifully the terrace grew from nothing; and the white umbrellas grew like blue and white mushrooms. Saying 'Carlsberg Lager'.

'An a butler, an' maids . . .'

They opened the front door and came out on to the terrace; dressed in black and white, like something out of an old Hollywood movie.

Sharon looked for Darren. He had crept up behind Warren; and was sitting on the ground, cross-legged, listening to everything Warren was saying, with a naughty smile on his face. You could tell he was *teasing* Warren, by building up this building for him. No malice, just three-year-old, or five-year-old, or ten-year-old's fun.

But she knew how cruel such fun could be; without meaning to be. She knew that such fun could *destroy* Warren. That if he knew that Darren could do such things . . .

'Darren! Stop that!' she said sharply.

Warren whirled round, to see what Darren was doing.

But as he did so, the whole building vanished, and the moor just stood as it had before. With a few crows flying where the building had been.

'What was he doin'?' asked Warren.

'Mucking around with a bee,' she lied.

Darren just stood grinning at them, unrepentant. Having his bit of childish fun. But she knew something in that instant, as sure as she had ever known anything.

Warren was not Darren's father. Darren was fond of Warren; but Darren didn't owe him *love*. Not like he loved his dear little mummy dear . . . When Warren had said he hadn't got her pregnant, hadn't gone too far, he'd been speaking the truth. Like he always had. It filled her with a great love for Warren, that he'd still wanted her, still married her. A great *protective* love. For in future, she knew she would have to protect him against Darren.

As for Darren . . . she remembered that night in the wood, the bright light, the tinkling music, the falling asleep. Darren was a magic child, a faerie child. He was growing tall, but he was oddly slender for his age. He had that silken-haired, blue-eyed beauty that had little to do with her, and nothing to do with Warren.

But he was hers, and she was his. He didn't grin at her; he smiled the cool smile that said dear little mummy dear.

They moved house again; at least the new one had two acres of paddock, so they could take the goat and the hens and the cats with them. And the photograph of the old lady. Sharon hung it on the wall, as soon as they got to the new house; the old lady was kind of honorary grandmother now. She still smiled at Sharon, and made Sharon feel safe.

Warren had talked of buying a house; but Sharon got him

to see that there was no point; as Darren grew, they would soon have to move again.

'Look,' said Warren one night, glancing up from checking his Filofax. 'What gives with that kid? I mean he looks like a six year old. The woman next door asked me what school he was going to . . .'

She sighed. So it had got through to Warren at last. It had taken an unbelievably long time, even allowing for Warren hardly ever being home before Darren went to bed, and Warren's excitement at being made a full manager, and Warren's total ignorance of children.

'I mean,' said Warren, a bit cross at being dragged away from the amount the firm was making selling insurance, all detailed in his Filofax, 'is he a *freak* or something? I got up to the lav one night last week an' he was sitting on my study floor, reading a book about insurance that *I* can't understand.'

'What did you say to him?' Her heart was in her mouth.

'I just carried him back to bed.'

Oh, thank God for Warren's simple goodness.

'Well,' asked Warren again, '*is* he a freak, or what?'

Behind Warren's back, Darren had drifted in through the open door. His striped pyjamas were drooping round his bottom. He yawned. He looked sleepy and adorable. Except his eyes were searching on Sharon's face.

Am I a freak, dear little mummy dear?

And it reminded her of a pigeon, that had once landed on their window-sill at home. As big as a grown-up pigeon, very strong and beautiful. But it couldn't fly properly. It didn't seem to know how to use its wings. She'd thought it was hurt, till its mother had come to take it away. It had just been very young; very strong but very young.

Darren was very strong, but very young. He had magic powers, but he didn't really understand them himself. He was some sort of . . . god? Angel? But he was a baby as well. And he was frightened . . . if she let Warren call him a freak . . .

She took Warren's hand. She spoke to him softly. But she was really speaking to Darren.

'Look, he's what they call a prodig ... prodigy. An infant prodigy.'

'What's one of those?' asked Warren, suspiciously. 'You mean he's not *normal?*'

'No ... normal. But there aren't very many of them. Children who are geniuses. There was a child called Mozart ... we learnt about him at school. He started playing the piano when he was two; he was making up songs at three, giving concerts at four ... all over the world.'

'Oh,' said Warren. 'What group's he with?'

'This was hundreds of years ago ...'

'Oh.' Warren's attention was starting to drift back to the rows of figures of profit-growth in his Filofax. 'Good. Great. Well, our infant genius better start going to school. I told you that *months* ago, Sharon ...'

'I'll see to it,' she said, breathing thanks to whatever gods there be. She had seen Darren smile at her over Warren's shoulder, and drift away quite satisfied.

She found a school. A posh private school, which didn't ask to see Darren's birth certificate, once they had seen Warren's cheque for the first term's fees.

The first morning, she took him to the gate of the playground. He was excited, trembling like a greyhound before a race, at the sight of all the kids running about mauling each other, in a polite sort of way, much hampered by grey blazers and grey caps and proper school satchels on their backs.

'Now remember,' she told him. 'You have to *pretend*. Pretend you're *seven*. Right? And pretend you don't know all the answers. And don't answer too many of the teacher's questions. Or you'll get called a swot, and the other boys won't like you. Watch them; do everything the way they do it. Right?'

Then, heart in mouth like any mother, she left him. And went home and wept her eyes out. Then wiped her eyes, put on fresh make-up and went for her driving-lesson.

Darren's first day seemed to go well. By the time she met him at the school gate, he'd learnt to slouch in the approved way, pull his cap down right over his eyes, talk out of the corner of his mouth, complain about the school dinner custard and other seven-year-old essentials. As day followed day, she began to worry less.

Until the day before half-term.

She got to the yard. The kids weren't trailing out to the cars as usual, with their little grey shirts drooping outside their shorts. Instead, there was a vast ring of kids, mums and teachers round something invisible by the porch.

Terrified, she ran across.

There was a very little boy standing sobbing to his mum. His cap was gone, his blazer torn, the blood was streaming from his nose in bubbles. But even he kept glancing at a much stranger sight.

Two of the bigger boys were floating in the air, about two feet from the ground. They waved their arms and legs frantically about, but could grab hold of nothing. They were red-faced, screaming, terrified. Teachers and mums kept trying to grab them; but for some reason they couldn't. It was as if the floating boys were surrounded by an invisible wall.

Most of the kids were pale, paralysed with fright, mouths open. Like most of the teachers and mums.

Only Darren stood, one hand in his pocket, gently smiling. If anyone had had eyes to see, he would've stuck out like a sore thumb. Luckily, all eyes were on the floating boys.

In the distance, sirens began sounding. Getting nearer. Official help was on its way; in a moment, it would be an official matter.

She sidled up to Darren, as quietly as she could on shaking legs. Took him by the shoulder, as if offering him protection he didn't need.

'That's enough!' she said sharply. 'Darren, *enough*.'

The two floating, screaming boys hit the playground with dull thuds. Their mums grabbed them. The screaming faded to sobs.

A Panda screeched into the playground. Followed by an ambulance and a fire engine. Two policemen pushed their way through.

'What's all this, then?'

The amazing thing, Sharon thought afterwards, was how all the teachers and parents began covering up, pretending nothing had really happened. The headmaster led the two policemen away to his study for a chat. The two mums got their sobbing offspring into their cars like greased lightning. The rest got away nearly as quickly, before they got involved with the police. Only the ambulance men stood around with the firemen in the empty yard, wondering what on earth was going on.

God, how the middle class hated getting involved with the police. Though Sharon reckoned that, once home, they'd be burning the telephone lines to each other for *hours*.

She walked Darren home, holding his hand *very* firmly, in spite of his protests that she was making him look like a baby in front of all of his mates.

She got him indoors and said '*Well?*' She felt like *hitting* him, for giving her such a fright. But she knew she'd better not. If she ever broke his trust . . .

He looked at her, cool as ever.

'Those two were bullying Simon Waterson. They punched him in the face. They were twisting his arm. They tore his blazer. They're always at him; and he's my mate . . .'

'You hadn't thought of punching them instead?' she said sarcastically.

'I don't believe in violence,' he said. And went up to his room to do his homework. She sat and shivered. It was the sharp, clipped way he had said *violence*. She suddenly had a vision of what violence *he* held in his hand.

The school lasted a year; which was longer than she had dared to hope; though the remarks about his growth had been pretty pointed at the last parents' meeting. He now looked and moved like a wiry ten year old. And he cycled in four times a week to the public library. He kept on bringing books home from the adult section, on physics and geology and words too hard for her to pronounce. The books weren't stamped by the library with the date, either. He must be stealing them. She had her sharpest words with him yet. Obediently, he stopped going to the library.

But the books kept appearing in his bedroom just the same. They still weren't stamped with the date . . .

She supposed it wasn't really stealing; they vanished again, once he'd read them.

Then one day the headmaster summoned her. She drove down trembling. (She had passed her test by then, and Warren had bought her a Fiat Panda; the firm had given him an Audi Quattro.)

But the Head was not distressed. The Head was in ecstasy.

'We have a genius on our hands, Mrs Slingsby! I was taking Darren's class, teaching them about the atom. Your young genius took issue with me about protons (my own degree is in physics, of course). I'm pleased to say he had me tied up in knots. We came into my study afterwards for a chat. Did you know there's an organization for helping the parents of highly gifted children . . . I'd like to contact them . . . tests . . .'

'I'm sorry,' she said, tight-lipped. 'We're moving next week – I meant to let you know – my husband's work . . .'

They moved again. But she was beginning to grow desperate.

He stayed at home. He watched TV all day, when he wasn't reading the books that appeared in his bedroom. (The books got thicker and thicker. She couldn't understand a word they said. Even when they weren't in German or Latin. With some, she couldn't even recognize the *letters* that made up the words.) He watched TV, with his long gangling teenage legs stretched across the hearthrug.

He was actually four years old.

They were very much alone, now. Increasingly, Warren was swallowed up by the world of business. Mostly, when he was home, he played squash and tennis with Darren. They had their own tennis-court, their own squash-court. They were stinking rich. If Sharon had had any worry to spare, she would have worried about the income-tax man. But she had no worry to spare.

Warren never commented on Darren now: on his size, on his always staying at home. She knew Darren had taken away, gently, that part of Warren's mind. The neighbours never made remarks about Darren, either, even when they came in for drinks. They had their own kids to worry about; kids who got drunk, went on drugs, got expelled from school, crashed their fathers' cars. All the neighbours said was how quiet and polite Darren was. She felt they envied her.

They were all sitting together one night when Warren switched on the six o'clock news. The one when the news from Ismailia broke. The camera-crews had got into Ismailia at last, and they had done their job thoroughly. The pictures were hideous. A million people were being deliberately starved to death by the dictator Makenza. There was an endless agonizing panorama of starving children's faces. There was the dictator Makenza, fat and loathsome in his bemedalled uniform. There were Makenza's security police, horrible as insects in their paratroopers' spotted jackets and dark glasses, waving guns like pop-stars waved guitars.

Even Warren left his Filofax and stared paralysed; he broke out in a sweat, and kept saying, 'Christ, oh *Christ*,' and helping himself to whisky from the sideboard.

Sharon just cowered down in her chair, overwhelmed by it all. Saying, 'Please, no! Please, *no*!' She wanted to get up and turn it off; but pain held her paralysed. She didn't even *look* at Darren, till it was all over, and a programme about growing alpine plants mercifully replaced it.

It was only then that Darren spoke. And he spoke like a four year old.

'Why don't they *stop* Makenza, Mum?'

She looked at him. In the dim glow of the TV, tears were running down his face. His whole face was wet and working with them.

'It's the way the world is, son,' said Warren wretchedly.

'We can't do nothing. They won't let the relief-teams through. They attack Unicef convoys an' kill the drivers.'

'Right,' said Darren, wiping his face with his cuff. 'I'm going up to my room.'

They heard his stereo start up. His favourite classical record; Wagner's 'Ride of the Valkyrie'. But they'd never heard him play it so long; or so loud. He was normally a thoughtful child, who played his records quietly. Now the hunting, riding theme filled the whole house. Over and over. Till they grew afraid to go upstairs, and cowered again in their chairs.

At ten precisely, he stopped. Came downstairs and switched the TV on again.

'Oh, don't, Darren,' Sharon whispered. 'I couldn't bear to see it again.'

But it wasn't seen again. The ten o'clock news was a shambles; a hysterical shambles of announcers having bits of paper shoved under their noses, and receiving unexpected phone-calls from our correspondents on the spot.

The impregnable fortress where Makenza dwelt seemed to have vanished in a vast explosion.

Makenza's beetle-soldiers were lying dead in heaps all over the place, dead from a cause unknown.

Vast unexplained mountains of corn had appeared in the famine areas.

The relief-teams were getting through.

Warren departed the following morning, into a world that would do no business that day, because it was talking about Ismailia. Incredible bits of newsreel kept on flooding the newsrooms. Talking heads talked non-stop all day, trying to make sense of explosions that had hurt no innocent person; an unknown plague that wiped out only soldiers; piles of corn that were rapidly diminishing as the starving million moved in.

Darren watched it all, lying in his chair, listless, depressed. Sharon tempted him with drinks, apple-pies, even his favourite, peanut butter on white toast. He wanted nothing.

And as she talked and talked, the silence between them grew and grew.

At last, as dusk closed in, and she drew the long curtains, he stirred and said,

'Where did I come from, Mum?'

She reached across and held his hand, and wept. Then told him about the night in the wood, and the brilliant light, and the tinkling music. When she had finished, she said, 'So Warren's not really your Dad . . .'

'I knew that,' he said wearily. Then added, 'But you're my Mum, aren't you?'

He sounded so lonely, she wept harder.

'I don't know what to do, Mum. I don't belong here. I'm too *big.*'

She grabbed him and cuddled him, like she hadn't done since he was small.

'You can stay, Darren. You'll just have to learn to pretend better, that's all.'

'I can't pretend, Mum. Not about Ismailia. Not like I could about school . . .'

'You mustn't do that kind of thing again, Darren. It'd drive people *mad.*'

'I know, Mum. That's why I've got to go. But *where?* Who were they? Why did they leave me here? I keep reading books, but there's never anything about *them* in them. About *me.*'

He seemed so lost, so quietly desperate.

She said, 'I'll show you the place, if you like. I think I can remember where it is.'

They went together, sitting side by side, in her Fiat Panda. She found the wood; she found the very place, because there was a twisted hawthorn tree, with a squiggle on its trunk that looked like an old witch's face. She even lay down for him, where she had lain with Warren.

He lay beside her; nearly as tall as Warren had been. He was silent a long time. Then he said, 'Yes, they were here. I can still feel them.' And after a bit he said, 'I can feel the way they went.' And after a much longer time, he said, 'I can almost reach them. Where they are.' And then his hand suddenly reached for hers, in the dark. His hand was shaking, but his voice wasn't lost any more. 'I've found them. They're coming for me.'

'Who are they, Darren? What do they want with you? Why did they give you to me?' And then, hopelessly, 'Why are they taking you away again?'

His voice was gentle, in the dusk. 'I . . . just . . . can't explain . . . dear little mummy dear. It's too difficult. Except that they are . . . cold, cold. They had forgotten how to . . . *feel*. You . . . taught me to *feel*. For Warren. For Simon. For Ismailia. That's why they picked you.'

'Take me with you, Darren . . . *please*. There's nothing here, without you.'

'There's Warren. Warren loves you.'

'Does he?' she asked, dully. It was more than she could bear. 'Why can't I come with *you*?'

'You couldn't live, where I'm going. You couldn't breathe. You'd go mad with loneliness. It's so *cold*, out there.' He shuddered. 'I hope I can stand it.'

To comfort him, she held his hand again. Like when he was little.

He said, a little shakily, 'I can make your life very happy. I can make you forget me. So you can be happy with Warren . . .'

'I don't want to forget you . . . ever.' She clung to him with every ounce of her strength. And he held her.

She had her eyes shut. But that didn't stop the silver light, the unstoppable silver light, prising in through her tight-squeezed lids. That didn't stop the silvery music creeping in through her ears.

'They've come,' he said gently, loosening her hands. 'I must go. They can't wait long.'

'Oh, Darren.'

'Goodbye, dear little mummy dear. Be happy if you can.'

And then there was only the woods and the darkness, and the little Fiat Panda.

She lay a long time, in the quiet dark, and thought. Thought of the beginning. How she and Warren had been forced away from their friends by their love, out into the woods alone. Had it all been planned by Them, even down to her Giro cheque not arriving that morning? The way she'd lost her Mum and Dad, by the pregnancy, and Warren's family by their own growing wealth. How Warren had been drawn away by work and money and squash and Country Club . . . leaving her to bring Darren to the place where he started and where he finished. Had They planned everything?

And what was she going to do with the rest of her life? The thought was unthinkable . . .

Then the thought came into her mind, from nowhere, glowing like a bright joyous spark.

Go *home*, dear little mummy dear. Go home to Warren. Warren's free to love you now.

He was still with her, through all the years.

It would be all right.

The Badger

I have interviewed the accused. He was co-operative. But he was very difficult to get settled down. First he asked for the curtains of the window to be drawn; though it was brilliant sunshine outside. Then he noticed the door of the interview-room was ajar. He insisted not only that it be shut, but locked. (I brought the constable on duty into the room with us before I locked the door.) Even that did not seem to satisfy the accused. His eye was constantly on the window, checking for chinks in the curtains, through which somebody or something might be watching him. He would not believe the constable had really locked the door behind him. Even when I let him check it for himself, he insisted on re-checking it every few minutes. He finally insisted that we leave the ground floor altogether. To humour him, I took him up to the third floor, which has a fine commanding view of the town. But even here, the curtain-drawing and door-locking rituals persisted.

You will gather from this that the accused is acutely disturbed; I will go further, and say he is in a state of terror. I know this is common in men accused of murder. But this terror showed none of the normal symptoms. He shows no sign of guilt or remorse; he seems indifferent to the fate of his victims. He shows no fear of punishment, even of a life-sentence. He appears to want no more than to remain locked away for the rest of his life. His only complaint is that the imprisonment is not secure enough. He kept on asking me anxiously which prisons were maximum-security – he has a great fear of what he called 'open' prisons.

When I asked him what he was afraid of, he would not

answer. But as I continued to talk to him, his fearful glances at the window and the door, his constant starting up and pacing, caused in me the growing conviction that there was something dreadful outside waiting to get in. I found this increasingly oppressive. I observed a similar unease growing in the constable who accompanied us. Yet I know PC Stevens to be the steadiest of men. I must say that even as I write this, in my own office, the conviction of some dreadful thing outside remains, and is only slowly fading. I have never in all my long professional life known anything like it.

I fear for the accused's sanity; I fear for the sanity of any warder or social worker who spends too much time with him, so great is the power of his delusion.

But to return to more mundane matters. The accused is James Long, of 22, Brownleigh Avenue, Croxteth, Liverpool. He has seven previous convictions; two are for grievous bodily harm, and the rest are concerned with badger-digging. He is forty-eight years old, of a wiry muscular build, and gives the impression of being a hardened criminal and a very nasty man in a fight. Both convictions for grievous bodily harm resulted from attacks on passers-by who tried to interfere with his badger-digging activities.

He states quite unequivocally that his policy was to put the passers-by out of action for long enough to facilitate the escape of his badger-digging gang, before the local police could be informed. He said it was 'inconvenient' to be caught. The usual fine for badger-digging – £200 – did not worry him, as he frequently was paid £500 for a live badger by contacts in Liverpool, who needed them for staged badger-baitings.

But arrest meant the confiscation of all his badger-digging tools . . .

He dates the beginning of the circumstances that led up to the crime with which he is charged from a badger-digging expedition to Delamere Forest across the Mersey in Cheshire. They had chosen a wet Monday evening, because they thought the forest, a well-frequented local beauty-spot, would be empty.

They knew the forest well, and had already located most of the badger-sets. But the evening had gone badly. Two terriers had been seriously mauled, and when they dug down to the badger, and got it out with the irons, it was visibly dying from its wounds. The accused admitted that he finished it off with a diagonal blow to the head with a spade, not to spare the beast suffering, but out of pure pique.

It was at this point that they realized that they were being observed. The accused looked up and saw a man watching them. He was very tall and thin, with dark hair and spectacles, and from the track-suit he was wearing, the accused thought he was a jogger. The accused tried to bluff the man by walking across to him, explaining they were working for a local farmer, gassing foxes. He admits he hoped to get close enough to the man to injure him sufficiently so that he could not raise the alarm before the gang escaped. But the man had evidently summed up the situation at a glance, and ran off along one of the forest tracks. The accused tried pursuit; but the man was obviously an experienced runner and very quickly left the accused behind.

It was also obvious to the accused that the man was making for the nearest house with a telephone, which was less than a mile away. (The forest is a large and lonely place.) At the speed the man was moving, the accused thought he would reach the house in just over five minutes; they could expect Pandas at the scene in less than a quarter of an hour. This made their situation desperate indeed, as there is only one road skirting the forest, and their car was the only one parked on it that night. Encumbered with tools, and two injured terriers, they could not hope to reach the car in time to get clear. The accused suggested that they kill the terriers, which were covered in blood, and hide the bodies; but the terriers' owner objected because of their expense; and the accused was reluctant anyway to abandon his tools. However, he states he thought 'they had had it'.

When they reached their car, they were surprised to find no police-car near it. The accused sent out a companion who had little blood on him, to drive the car up and down the road, to check that the police were not lying in wait at the end of it. The accomplice returned after quarter of an hour, saying that the road was completely clear and no Pandas were in sight. The three of them piled aboard, putting the injured dogs, their own bloodstained outer garments and the badger-irons in the boot and locking it. Then they drove off. The general feeling was that the jogger had failed to find the householder with the phone at home, and that they had had a lucky escape.

However, the accused states that while they were waiting for the car, he had a distinct feeling of being watched from the shadowy mass of the forest, which left him uneasy. He said that afterwards, this feeling of 'being watched' seldom left him, and slowly increased. I have no doubt that this feeling of 'being watched' is the root of all his present fear and delusion.

The accused states he dropped his accomplices and drove home to Brownleigh Avenue. Perhaps a description of the house may be helpful at this point. Brownleigh Avenue is a respectable road of substantial semis with large front and rear gardens, usually well kept. It dates from the 1930s and there are brick-built garages. It could be described as 'leafy', with a grass verge and a row of mature trees between the pavement and the road. Most of the front gardens have a lawn. But the accused had encouraged his wife, who is a keen gardener, to plant the front garden with conifers, which have now grown to a considerable height. They are densely clumped, and most are over six feet high. Together with a six-foot privet hedge, they totally hide the house from the road. The back garden is similarly planted, though there is a small central lawn. The overall effect is to make the house rather dark and very private. It no doubt suited the accused to have his activities well hidden from his neighbours, who are all respectable people. I have made enquiries of the neighbours. The accused is quarrelsome and not liked; over the years, the neighbours have come to ignore him as 'not one of us' though they know nothing against him, and he is taken at face-value as a steel-erector, the trade he follows by day.

*

The following evening, the accused returned home from work and was met by his wife complaining that some dog had dug a hole in the front garden. On inspecting the hole, he formed the opinion that the hole had been dug not by a dog, but by a badger. That it was, in fact, the beginning of a badger-set. He is quite definite about this. He says that after thirty years of badger-digging, he knows the marks of a badger's paws, and I am inclined to believe him. However, the hole at that time, he says, was very small; so perhaps there is room for doubt. In any case, it did not worry him at that stage; in fact he joked to his accomplices that soon they would not need to drive into Cheshire; the badgers would be coming to him.

He persuaded his wife to leave the hole, which grew bigger over the week.

Then, however, on the Saturday night, after a heavy drinking-spree, he left his car out in the drive overnight, as he was afraid he might damage it getting it into the very narrow garage.

On the Sunday morning, he slept late; his wife aroused him at eleven, going on about the state of the car.

The car is an old Ford Granada, off-white in colour. The accused was very proud of it, and kept it well polished. But that morning, he states it was covered with black muddy pawmarks from end to end. His wife was inclined to blame the neighbour's large black tom-cat. But the accused could readily distinguish the marks of a badger's paws again, which had not only left prints, but scratched the enamel quite badly in places.

The accused admits to becoming uneasy at that point. Whereas the hole in the garden seemed 'natural' to him, the attack on the car did not. There seemed to him something 'personal' in it. He made inquiries of the neighbours, as to whether anyone had ever seen traces of a badger. No one had, though there were some reports of hedgehogs being fed saucers of milk, rabbits being seen on lawns, and a fox living beneath a garden shed. The back gardens of the area are quite extensive, and some are neglected and overgrown.

He also says that his sense of being 'watched' increased. He re-polished his car, and never left it out overnight again.

It did him little good. Three nights later, the green wooden doors of his garage were found to be heavily scratched, and wood at the bottom was broken away in places, where it was slightly rotten.

Again, the marks of a badger's powerful claws were quite clear. He formed the opinion that the beast had been attracted first to the car, and then to the garage doors by the smell coming from the car-boot. He had, in his time, carried many caged live badgers in that boot. Perhaps this new free beast could still smell them ... The following evening, he washed out both the boot and the interior of the car with strong disinfectant.

It made a difference. The following morning, it was the front door of the house that had suffered; the clawmarks were scored deep into the wood, and it looked very unsightly. His wife insisted that he dealt with the problem, before the whole look of the house was ruined.

. That was the first night he sat up with a shot-gun. He stayed awake until five, sitting at the foot of the stairs. Then, as the sky began to grey, he dozed off ...

He came awake to the sound of something attacking the wood of the front door. It took him several moments to realize he wasn't asleep in bed and dreaming. A few more to fumble getting the front door open; and the massive clawing had stopped before he did so.

He peered out into a bleak dawn, and an empty drive. But there was something lying on the metal foot-scraper in front of the door. An object about the size of a small rat, but streaked with coarse grey, black and white hairs. As he picked it up, the stench of rotting flesh hit him full up the nostrils. Then when he turned it over, he saw what it was. A badger's paw. It squelched rottenly in his hand, oozing a vile juice. It had been dead a long time; the hairs were stripping off as he held it. He made a sound of disgust, and was just about to put it in the dustbin, when he saw the new clawmarks on his front door. Very large clawmarks indeed. Somebody must have used this dead claw to make the marks ... what sort of crazy bugger ...?

Dumbly he tried to fit the rotting paw into the new claw-marks. But they wouldn't fit. The dead paw was far too small, its claws too close together . . . yet he knew it was the paw of a normal fully-grown badger. The creature that had made these deep wounds in the hardwood must have been a giant. Twice the usual size. For God's sake, how big?

And again, he had that sense of being watched. Beside himself with rage, he prowled round the garden, gun at the ready.

But he found nothing. He rushed out into the road, and thought he saw the boot and back wheels of a car, just turning away round the corner into the main road. But that meant bugger-all; probably just some bastard on the early shift going to work. He cast an eye over next-door's garden, on both sides. Nothing. Still that uncanny sense of being watched . . .

That was the first time he admitted to feeling afraid. He ran into the house, and slammed the door behind him, and listened to the sound of his own harsh breathing.

It is hard to fathom what his state of mind was at this time. I would judge him to be a successful psychopath. That is, he is not without wit, and had a great deal of nous and low cunning. Being a psychopath, as I said before, he is incapable of feeling guilt or remorse. And he had shown in the past a great deal of physical courage. He was used to solving his problems by calculated violence, and did not mind the risk of getting hurt in the process. I asked him what he thought was happening at that time. He said he thought he was dealing with a huge, violent and cunning badger – probably a boar in mating-rut who had formed the idea that he was keeping a female badger in his house. He asked his acquaintances about the biggest badgers they had ever known. He went so far as to visit the public library for the first time in his life, to ask for books about both foreign and English badgers.

He said after that, things went quiet for a week. On the Monday night, he led another hunt for badgers, again to

The Badger

Delamere Forest. I think he had some idea of 'getting his own back' on the badger that was persecuting him.

The hunt went disastrously wrong; they had scarcely begun digging when the Cheshire police turned up in strength. There was no point in making a fight of it. He lost all his badger-digging tools. He began to get a superstitious feeling that 'his luck was running out'. It was to test this, I think, that he led another raid three nights later.

He was caught again. He did not get home till three in the morning, to find his wife hysterical. Lying awake, waiting for his return, she had heard 'something like a large animal' moving around through the bushes in the garden. She had gone as far as opening the front door and shining a torch among the bushes; but the heavy and violent way the bushes had moved had scared her back indoors. Later, she had heard scraping 'against the wall of the house'. She had been tempted to ring the police, but had been afraid to, because of questions they might ask.

Perhaps a word about the wife might be appropriate here. She is a well-muscled and large woman; a little younger than her husband. Hard-faced, with peroxided hair. She had taken no part in his badger-digging activity, but he states 'she knew something was going on'. She had remarked on badger-hairs and bloodstains, both in the boot of the car, and occasionally in the car itself. She had become used to receiving 'presents' of up to a hundred pounds in notes, after a successful 'hunt'. This money she spent on 'things for the house and garden'. The house was opulently furnished, in a vulgar way – large colour TV, videotape recorder (seldom used), hi-fi and cocktail bar and a large and ugly three-piece suite. There was a large and ill-drawn print of badgers over the fireplace, and when he gave her a 'present' they used to 'drink to the badgers'.

At any rate, he immediately 'did the rounds' of the house walls, with a torch in one hand, and his gun in the other. What he found frightened him further. The house had a sprung wooden floor, with a half-cellar beneath, and airbricks set in the wall to ventilate the half-cellar. One air-brick had been entirely ripped-out, and there were clawmarks on the surrounding bricks. The overall hole was nearly a foot in diameter. There were badger-hairs, black and grey and very coarse, on the outside of the hole, but not on the inside. The beast had tried to get through the hole, and failed. This implied a size . . .

His wife told him straight. He must get rid of the beast, or she would leave home. He seems at this time to have thought about calling in official help from the council. He went as far as ringing the environmental health department. But they began to ask questions, and he was afraid of officials asking questions. He rang off, without giving his name and address. Besides, he saw it as a personal fight; it was him or the badger. He took the following day off work, and repaired the hole in the wall with bricks and cement, while his wife went to work. That night, he sat up again with his gun, in the open porch of his house with the front door closed behind him. He heard and saw nothing; until at two a.m., he heard his wife screaming inside the house. He rushed in to find her half-way up the stairs. She had awakened to hear heavy scratching and scraping on wood, inside the house itself. She thought it was coming from the dining-room. On going into the dining-room, he saw the fitted carpet was raised in a low hump against one side of the wall. On pulling up the carpet, he found two floorboards pushed upwards about two inches and loose of their nails.

He went outside again, beside himself with rage. He found the hole he had repaired the previous day untouched. But on going round to the back of the house, he found another air-brick had been pulled out, and an even larger hole made; a hole big enough to admit a grown man. He says he almost failed to spot it; it was hidden by some ferns that grew up to the wall, about three feet high.

Neither he nor his wife slept again that night. They sat up till daylight, drinking tea in the kitchen.

When the sun was fully up, he crawled into the new hole. (This is not quite so crazy as it sounds – the man had a 'sense'

of badgers. He says he 'sensed' the creature had long gone.)
On entering the hole, he was appalled by the stink of badger.
What frightened him most was that it was not the smell of a
living badger, but the stink of a long-dead and decaying one.
He found many badger-hairs both round the entrance-hole,
and among the brick-rubble of the floor. And the underside of
the lifted floorboards were marked by claws of unbelievable
strength. The inch-thick floorboards were reduced to half their
original thickness, and the splinters of wood covered a large
area.

To complete his misery, he saw light pouring into the half-
cellar from the front wall as well. On examination, he found
that his work of filling that hole the previous day had been
utterly destroyed. He came to the conclusion that while he
had been examining the hole at the back, the creature had
been reopening the hole at the front.

By this time, he was very badly shaken. I think the delusions
which now haunt him stem from this point. He abandoned his
theory that this was any kind of living badger, however
exotic, foreign and large. He formed an image of a beast of
superhuman strength and superhuman cunning; and also,
much worse, a beast that was 'dead'.

He began to brood on all the badgers he had killed or sent to
their deaths in the badger-baiting ring all those years he had
been working the game. Still, being what he is, he felt no
remorse, or guilt. But he knew now the thing was stronger
and cleverer than him, and that it wanted revenge for the
deaths. Revenge was an emotion he understood all too well.
The beast was hunting him to kill him, and he knew how it
meant to kill him. The savage deep clawmarks in wood and
brick told him all too clearly. For the first time in his life, he
was the hunted, not the hunter.

He did not tell any of this to his wife; but his new fear was
contagious. His wife said she would not be left alone in the
house till the beast was found and killed. If he left the house,
she would pack and leave immediately.

The next three days must have been hell for them both.

They had reached that state in marriage which is only-tolerable when the couple do not see much of each other. She had long ago insisted on separate bedrooms. He had had other women, but she neither knew nor cared. Most of the time he was at work, or badger-digging, or drinking with his cronies. She had her garden and her house; of both of which she was very proud. She cooked his meals and did his washing. To her, he was a pay-packet. They had no interests in common; they seldom exchanged more than a few words. In a practical way, they needed each other; but if there had ever been love, it was long gone.

The neighbours heard them quarrelling. They heard him, on the third night, leave the house, banging the front door violently.

Half an hour later, they heard her screaming. They ran around to see what was the matter. She did not answer the saccharine chimes of the doorbell. But the screaming and sobbing was quite audible. In the end, the neighbour's husband, very reluctantly, broke in the front door with a kick. By that time, half the street was roused and round the front gate.

They were a long time in finding her; though the sobbing was still audible. In the end they found her in the upstairs airing-cupboard, with the doors pulled shut on herself. She was crammed in between the hot-water cistern and the wall, in a foetal position. The neighbours couldn't believe anyone bigger than a child could have crammed itself into such a small space.

They found it impossible to calm her; they became frightened themselves, and summoned first a doctor, and then the police. The doctor gave her a shot of something to calm her; the constable tried to question her. All he could get out of her was that she had been trying to draw the curtains on the dark front garden when she had seen a face rearing suddenly above the massed conifers. And it had not been a human face, but an animal's face . . . She continued in a state of terror; panicking when anyone left the room, though at least ten people were present most of the time. In the end, the constable (who handled the business very competently and compassionately)

73

got her to agree to go to her sister's. The neighbour's wife helped her pack (or rather did her packing for her) and the constable drove her across in his Panda. He saw her into her sister's flat. He said that the one thing that seemed to reassure her was that the flat was in a tower-block, and on the fifteenth floor. Even then, she insisted on the curtains being drawn, and checked them carefully for herself, in the same way as her husband was to do later. I have made inquiries; and she has not dared leave her sister's flat since, even in broad daylight. She has been recommended for treatment by a psychiatrist.

The accused appears to have returned to the house at about half past eleven, very drunk and, at first, inclined to be quarrelsome. But when the neighbours told him what his wife had said, especially about the 'face' in the garden, he became 'very pale and very silent'. It says a great deal, in face of how he had always quarrelled with them, that they felt 'very sorry' for him. They felt he was very frightened, and they found themselves infected by his fear. After a few minutes they left, not knowing what else they could do, and finding themselves compelled every so often to look at the window.

The accused says that nothing else happened that night; in the end he fell asleep on the bed upstairs, having locked his door and placed a chair and a chest of drawers against it. He did not go to work next day; but at about three p.m. he rang up his sister-in-law, asking to speak to his wife. She refused to come to the phone and speak to him. He began to grow uneasy as darkness fell, and locked all the doors and made sure the windows were shut. What seems to have worried him most was whether to draw the curtains or not. He was afraid of what he might see if he did not draw them; on the other hand, he was afraid of what he might fail to see if he did draw them. In the end, he drew all the curtains in the house, and switched all the lights on. He spent the next three hours prowling the house with a loaded shot-gun in his hand, drinking a succession of cans of lager from the fridge. Eventually, he must have drunk himself into a stupor on the couch.

At some time in the early morning, he was awakened by hearing his name called. Just the word 'Jimmy, Jimmy', over and over again. It took him some time to realize that the voice was outside the house. He said it sounded 'odd – not human'. He sat up, shivering. He felt he could not move. But the voice continued to call him, from just outside the window. In the end, the calling became unbearable. He walked across and drew back the curtains of the window, that looked out on the front garden.

At first, he could see nothing but the tops of the conifers blowing in the slight wind. But then, as he watched, a head emerged from among them. More than six feet off the ground, he said, because the tops of the conifers were that high. He could see it quite clearly, in the light of the window.

It was the head of a full-grown badger. One ear hung loose, cut half through. The half-closed eyes were those of an animal that was dead. And on the forehead was the deep deadly cut of a spade.

He recognized it as the animal he had killed. At the same time, he thought he caught a whiff of putrefaction, coming through the joints in the window where the ventilators open.

He says he pointed the gun that was still in his hand, and let fly with both barrels at the head. He says he saw bits of fur fly off it, and for a moment it vanished, and he thought wildly that he'd killed it again.

But then it reappeared; and he heard his name called again. 'Jimmy, Jimmy.'

He knew it was calling him out into the garden; and that sooner or later he would have to go. And then . . .

At that point, he seems to have fainted. When he came to himself, it was six o'clock, dawn was just breaking and there was no sign of the thing. But the stink of dead badger was in the room; and there were hairs on the broken glass of the window, and badger paw-prints everywhere.

The accused seems to have spent the next day drinking solidly. He says he could no longer think of anything else to do.

But meanwhile, his two confederates of Delamere Forest became worried about him. Or, certainly, worried about some money he owed them. They had not been in the pub, the night he had been drinking, and had not seen him for five days. They had tried all evening to ring him at home; but he had given up answering the phone. By closing-time, the landlord said, they were talking aggressively of going round to his house and getting the money out of him. It is obvious they went round to his house. It may be they found it in darkness. It may be they noticed the shattered window of the lounge, when no one replied to their ring on the bell; saw the curtains billowing out in the night breeze. It may be that, worried, they went up to the broken window and called to him softly,

'Jimmy, Jimmy!'

The whole street was wakened by the shot-gun blast.

Both were dead on arrival at Liverpool General.

As you know, sir, I am not any kind of believer in the supernatural. To me, it is an abdication of the logical mind in favour of the rubbish in the subconscious. In my police work, I have found there is always an explanation if you look hard enough. There are always loose ends, which, if you follow them up, unravel.

We have certain evidence to support the accused's story. I have seen the broken lounge window. Forensic have analysed the hairs found round it, and they are the hairs of a badger that has been dead for some time – decomposed skin is still attached to them. The paw-prints on the walls of the lounge were made by the forepaws of a normal-sized badger. On the other hand, the clawmarks on the brickwork and the underside of the floorboards are three times the size, and forensic think they have found traces of mild steel in the gouge-marks which are not normally present in woodwork or brick. However, the traces are minimal, and there is no evidence how they got there.

I have managed to get the accused to give me an accurate description of the jogger he saw in Delamere Forest. I even persuaded him to come to the station, and work with the police artist in making an identikit portrait of the man. Indeed, the accused seemed pathetically eager to co-operate. I then had constables patrol the relevant paths of Delamere Forest at the relevant times in the evenings. For over two weeks, they drew a blank. But on the third Monday evening, such a jogger did turn up. He was tall and thin and dark; he wore spectacles, but otherwise bore little resemblance to the identikit picture. I have interviewed him. His name is Roger Harvey; he admitted quite freely that he was the jogger described by the accused.

Harvey states that he did run to the nearest house to try to phone for the police. Unfortunately, he took a wrong turning in the forest, and got to the wrong house where there was no phone. The householder remembers him calling, though he cannot remember at what time. After that, Harvey states he gave up, thinking the accused would be miles away by then.

Harvey admits to being a keen naturalist. He is a highly intelligent man, who took a degree in Zoology at Cambridge, getting a first, and then took a Ph.D. in animal behaviour, specializing in animal neurosis and its causes. He lectures in Biology in Mid-Cheshire Technical College, at Hartford, and is widely in demand with the local conservation groups for his evening talks on animal behaviour.

Among the groups he has lectured to is the local badger-defence group, who number about twenty.

I questioned him about his whereabouts on the relevant nights -- the night, for instance, when Mrs Long was terrified by the apparition in the garden, and the night after, when the accused saw the badger-head in the garden.

He has alibis for both nights, and for every other night in question – he has a very full diary. The alibis are invariably provided by members of the badger-protection group, who were either out with him on small nature-watching expeditions, or else entertaining him in the privacy of their own homes.

There is one more suggestive lead. I checked with the vehicle registration people at Swansea. On the day following the encounter in Delamere Forest, an enquiry was made about Long's vehicle registration, and his address obtained. The enquirer gave his name as Sergeant G. Brown, of Macclesfield Division. There is no Sergeant Brown listed in Macclesfield Division. But one of the badger-group, Henfield, is a special constable with Northwich Division, and would know the routine for getting an address out of Swansea.

I asked Harvey if I could meet his badger-group, as the case I was working on involved badgers, and I could use all the background information they could give me. I will say in their favour that they readily and willingly agreed to meet me.

You will know the type – middle aged and middle class. Scientists, teachers, accountants, a lawyer and a doctor. Very bright and as hard as nails, after a lifetime of getting what they want in a polite but ruthless way. Lean, blue-rinsed wives with trim figures from playing a lot of golf, with faces as ruthless as an American general's. They treated me with a bright nervous charm – but they always treat you with a bright nervous charm, even if you are lecturing them about Homewatch – it is their way of socializing, an elegant wall you can never hope to penetrate. And they had a feeling of group-solidarity and righteousness that would put the trade unions to shame. I knew before I started I wasn't going to get anywhere. They must have spent weeks working out their elaborate network of social alibis. And as they are constantly socializing in their shallow way, their behaviour over the past month would come out as absolutely normal.

What I got out of them was a lot of indignation about how the law punishes badger-diggers. As the chairman put it, 'Even when they're caught, they're only fined £200, when the law allows fines of £2000. £200 is nothing to them; £2000 would make them think twice, and £4000 a time would cripple them.'

With which viewpoint, I am inclined to agree.

Afterwards, they fed me with little savouries and drinks. Any other help they could give . . . I felt all the time they were laughing at me behind my back.

There is no doubt in my mind that they did take the law into their own hands with regard to Long. That they traced him home, and set out to teach him a lesson in terror, master-minded by Harvey, the animal behaviourist. Long, to them, was no more than an animal. It has always struck me that conservation-groups are fanatical, caring more for their protected species than for people. This group is exceptionally fanatical.

Of course, when they set out to teach him a lesson, they did not have murder on their minds. I don't know what they had on their minds, as they slowly and carefully drove him nuts. Perhaps they didn't know either. But now it's happened, they're totally unrepentant. I think they feel it's good riddance to bad rubbish, and they see no reason why their lives should be interrupted by criminal prosecution.

I feel I can carry my investigations no further, without your express orders. We should have to approach another police authority with strong allegations that we might not be able to prove. The group left me in no doubt about their connections – magistrates, county councillors; one or two know the Chief Constable himself. The fuss they could create if threatened would be enormous – and we could be left with nothing but a lot of egg on our faces. Nevertheless, they had the motive, the means (including one dead badger) and the opportunity.

You will note that this is not an official report, but a personal letter from me to you.

I await your further instructions.

The Call

I'm rota-secretary of our local Samaritans. My job's to see our office is staffed twenty-four hours a day, 365 days a year. It's a load of headaches, I can tell you. And the worst headache for any branch is overnight on Christmas Eve.

Christmas night's easy; plenty have had enough of family junketings by then; nice to go on duty and give your stomach a rest. And New Year's Eve's OK, because we have Methodists and other teetotal types. But Christmas Eve . . .

Except we had Harry Lancaster.

In a way, Harry *was* the branch. Founder-member in 1963. A marvellous director all through the sixties. Available on the phone, day or night. Always the same quiet, unflappable voice, asking the right questions, soothing over-excited volunteers.

But he paid the price.

When he took early retirement from his firm in '73, we were glad. We thought we'd see even more of him. But we didn't. He took a six-month break from Sams. When he came back, he didn't take up the reins again. He took a much lighter job, treasurer. He didn't look ill, but he looked *faded*. Too long as a Sam. director can do that to you. But we were awfully glad just to have him back. No one was gladder than Maureen, the new director. Everybody cried on Maureen's shoulder, and Maureen cried on Harry's when it got rough.

Harry was the kind of guy you wish could go on forever. But every so often, over the years, we'd realize he wasn't going to. His hair went snow-white; he got thinner and thinner. Gave up the treasurer-ship. From doing a duty once a week, he dropped to once a month. But we still *had* him. His presence was everywhere in the branch. The new directors, leaders, he'd trained them all. They still asked themselves in a tight spot, 'What would Harry do?' And what he did do was as good as ever. But his birthday kept on coming round. People would say with horrified disbelief, 'Harry'll be *seventy-four* next year!'

And yet, most of the time, we still had in our minds the fifty-year-old Harry, full of life, brimming with new ideas. We couldn't do without that dark-haired ghost.

And the one thing he never gave up was overnight duty on Christmas Eve. Rain, hail or snow, he'd be there. Alone.

Now alone is wrong; the rules say the office must be double-staffed at all times. There are two emergency phones. How could even Harry cope with both at once?

But Christmas Eve is hell to cover. Everyone's got children or grandchildren, or is going away. And Harry had always done it alone. He said it was a quiet shift; hardly anybody ever rang. Harry's empty log-book was there to prove it; never more than a couple of long-term clients who only wanted to talk over old times and wish Harry Merry Christmas.

So I let it go on.

Until, two days before Christmas last year, Harry went down with flu. Bad. He tried dosing himself with all kinds of things; swore he was still coming. Was *desperate* to come. But Mrs Harry got in the doctor; and the doctor was adamant. Harry argued; tried getting out of bed and dressed to prove he was O K. Then he fell and cracked his head on the bedpost, and the doctor gave him a shot meant to put him right out. But Harry, raving by this time, kept trying to get up, saying he must go . . .

But I only heard about that later. As rota-secretary I had my own troubles, finding his replacement. The rule is that if the rota-bloke can't get a replacement, he does the duty himself. In our branch, anyway. But I was already doing the seven-to-ten shift that night, then driving north to my parents.

Eighteen fruitless phone-calls later, I got somebody. Meg and Geoff Charlesworth. Just married; no kids.

When they came in at ten to relieve me, they were happy. Maybe they'd had a couple of drinks in the course of the evening. They were laughing; but they were certainly fit to drive. It is wrong to accuse them, as some did, later, of having had too many. Meg gave me a Christmas kiss. She'd wound a bit of silver tinsel through her hair, as some girls do at Christmas. They'd brought long red candles to light, and mince-pies to heat up in our kitchen and eat at midnight. It was just happiness; and it *was* Christmas Eve.

Then my wife tooted our car-horn outside, and I passed out of the story. The rest is hearsay; from the log they kept, and the reports they wrote, that were still lying in the in-tray the following morning.

They heard the distant bells of the parish church, filtering through the falling snow, announcing midnight. Meg got the mince-pies out of the oven, and Geoff was just kissing her, mouth full of flaky pastry, when the emergency phone went.

Being young and keen, they both grabbed for it. Meg won. Geoff shook his fist at her silently, and dutifully logged the call. Midnight exactly, according to his new watch. He heard Meg say what she'd been carefully coached to say, like Samaritans the world over.

'Samaritans – can I help you?'

She said it just right. Warm, but not gushing. Interested, but not *too* interested. That first phrase is all-important. Say it wrong, the client rings off without speaking.

Meg frowned. She said the phrase again. Geoff crouched close in support, trying to catch what he could from Meg's ear-piece. He said afterwards the line was very bad. Crackly, very crackly. Nothing but crackles, coming and going.

Meg said her phrase the third time. She gestured to Geoff that she wanted a chair. He silently got one, pushed it in behind her knees. She began to wind her fingers into the coiled telephone-cord, like all Samaritans do when they're anxious.

Meg said into the phone, 'I'd like to help if I can.' It was good to vary the phrase, otherwise clients began to think you were a tape-recording. She added, 'My name's Meg. What can I call *you*?' You never ask for their *real* name, at that stage; always what you can call them. Often they start off by giving a false name . . .

A voice spoke through the crackle. A female voice.

'He's going to kill me. I know he's going to kill me. When he comes back.' Geoff, who caught it from a distance, said it wasn't the phrases that were so awful. It was the way they were said.

Cold; so cold. And certain. It left no doubt in your mind he *would* come back and kill her. It wasn't a wild voice you could hope to calm down. It wasn't a cunning hysterical voice, trying to upset you. It wasn't the voice of a hoaxer, that to the trained Samaritan ear always has that little wobble in it, that might break down into a giggle at any minute and yet, till it does, must be taken absolutely seriously. Geoff said it was a voice as cold, as real, as hopeless as a tombstone.

'Why do you think he's going to kill you?' Geoff said Meg's voice was shaking, but only a little. Still warm, still interested.

Silence. Crackle.

'Has he threatened you?'

When the voice came again, it wasn't an answer to her question. It was another chunk of lonely hell, being spat out automatically; as if the woman at the other end was really only talking to herself.

'He's gone to let a boat through the lock. When he comes back, he's going to kill me.'

Meg's voice tried to go up an octave; she caught it just in time.

'Has he *threatened* you? What is he going to do?'

'He's goin' to push me in the river, so it looks like an accident.'

'Can't you swim?'

'There's half an inch of ice on the water. Nobody could live a minute.'

'Can't you get away . . . before he comes back?'

'Nobody lives within miles. And I'm lame.'

'Can't I . . . you . . . ring the police?'

Geoff heard a click, as the line went dead. The dialling tone resumed. Meg put the phone down wearily, and suddenly shivered, though the office was over-warm, from the roaring gas-fire.

'Christ, I'm so *cold*!'

Geoff brought her cardigan, and put it round her. 'Shall I ring the duty-director, or will you?'

'You. If you heard it all.'

Tom Brett came down the line, brisk and cheerful. 'I've not gone to bed yet. Been filling the little blighter's Christmas stocking . . .'

Geoff gave him the details. Tom Brett was everything a good duty-director should be. Listened without interrupting; came back solid and reassuring as a house.

'Boats don't go through the locks this time of night. Haven't done for twenty years. The old alkali steamers used to, when the alkali-trade was still going strong. The locks are only manned nine till five nowadays. Pleasure-boats can wait till morning. As if anyone would be moving a pleasure-boat this weather . . .'

'Are you *sure*?' asked Geoff doubtfully.

'Quite sure. Tell you something else – the river's nowhere near freezing over. Runs past my back-fence. Been watching it all day, 'cos I bought the lad a fishing-rod for Christmas, and it's not much fun if he can't try it out. You've been *had*, old son. Some Christmas joker having you on. Goodnight!'

'Hoax call,' said Geoff heavily, putting the phone down. 'No boats going through locks. No ice on the river. Look!' He pulled back the curtain from the office window. 'It's still quite warm out – the snow's melting, not even lying.'

Meg looked at the black wet road, and shivered again. 'That was no hoax. Did you think that voice was a hoax?'

'We'll do what the boss-man says. Ours not to reason why . . .'

He was still waiting for the kettle to boil, when the emergency phone went again.

The same voice.

'But he *can't* just push you in the river and get away with it!' said Meg desperately.

'He can. I always take the dog for a walk last thing. And there's places where the bank is crumbling and the fence's rotting. And the fog's coming down. He'll break a bit of fence, then put the leash on the dog, and throw it in after me. Doesn't matter whether the dog drowns or is found wanderin'. Either'll suit *him*. Then he'll ring the police an' say I'm missin' . . .'

'But why should he *want* to? What've you *done*? To deserve it?'

'I'm gettin' old. I've got a bad leg. I'm not much use to him. He's got a new bit o' skirt down the village . . .'

'But can't we . . .'

'All you can do for me, love, is to keep me company till he comes. It's lonely . . . That's not much to ask, is it?'

'Where *are* you?'

Geoff heard the line go dead again. He thought Meg looked like a corpse herself. White as a sheet. Dull dead eyes, full of pain. Ugly, almost. How she would look as an old woman, if life was rough on her. He hovered, helpless, desperate, while the whistling kettle wailed from the warm Samaritan kitchen.

'Ring Tom again, for Christ's sake,' said Meg, savagely.

Tom's voice was a little less genial. He'd got into bed and turned the light off . . .

'Same joker, eh? Bloody persistent. But she's getting her facts wrong. No fog where I am. Any where you are?'

'No,' said Geoff, pulling back the curtain again, feeling a nitwit.

'There were no fog-warnings on the late-night weather forecast. Not even for low-lying districts . . .'

'No.'

'Well, I'll try to get my head down again. But don't hesitate to ring if anything *serious* crops up. As for this other lady . . . if she comes on again, just try to humour her. Don't argue – just try to make a relationship.'

In other words, thought Geoff miserably, don't bother me with *her* again.

But he turned back to a Meg still frantic with worry. Who would not be convinced. Even after she'd rung the local British Telecom weather summary, and was told quite clearly the night would be clear all over the Eastern Region.

'I want to know where she *is*. I want to know where she's ringing from . . .'

To placate her, Geoff got out the large-scale Ordnance-Survey maps that some offices carry. It wasn't a great problem. The Ousam was a rarity; the only canalized river with locks for fifty miles around. And there were only eight sets of locks on it.

'These four,' said Geoff, 'are right in the middle of towns and villages. So it can't be *them*. And there's a whole row of Navigation cottages at Sutton's Lock, and I know they're occupied, so it can't be *there*. And this last one – Ousby Point – is right on the sea and its all docks and stone quays – there's no river-bank to crumble. So it's either Yaxton Bridge, or Moresby Abbey locks . . .'

The emergency phone rang again. There is a myth among old Samaritans that you can tell the quality of the incoming call by the sound of the phone-bell. Sometimes it's lonely, sometimes cheerful, sometimes downright frantic. Nonsense, of course. A bell is a bell is a bell . . .

But this ringing sounded so cold, so dreary, so dead, that for a second they both hesitated and looked at each other with dread. Then Meg slowly picked the phone up; like a bather hesitating on the bank of a cold grey river.

It was the voice again.

'The boat's gone through. He's just closing the lock gates. He'll be here in a minute . . .'

'What kind of boat is it?' asked Meg, with a desperate attempt at self-defence.

The voice sounded put-out for a second, then said, 'Oh, the

usual. One of the big steamers. The *Lowestoft*, I think. Aye, the lock-gates are closed. He's coming up the path. Stay with me, love. Stay with me . . .'

Geoff took one look at his wife's grey, frozen, horrified face, and snatched the phone from her hand. He might be a Samaritan; but he was a husband, too. He wasn't sitting and watching his wife being screwed by some vicious hoaxer.

'Now *look*!' he said. 'Whoever you are! We want to help. We'd like to help. But stop feeding us lies. I know the *Lowestoft*. I've been aboard her. They gave her to the Sea-scouts, for a headquarters. She hasn't got an engine any more. She's a hulk. She's never moved for years. Now let's cut the cackle . . .'

The line went dead.

'Oh, *Geoff*!' said Meg.

'Sorry. But the moment I called her bluff, she rang off. That *proves* she's a hoaxer. All those old steamers were broken up for scrap, except the *Lowestoft*. She's a *hoaxer*, I tell you!'

'Or an old lady who's living in the past. Some old lady who's muddled and lonely and frightened. And you shouted at her . . .'

He felt like a murderer. It showed in his face. And she made the most of it.

'Go out and find her, Geoff. Drive over and see if you can find her . . .'

'And leave you alone in the office? Tom'd have my guts for garters . . .'

'Harry Lancaster always did it alone. I'll lock the door. I'll be all right. Go on, Geoff. She's lonely. Terrified.'

He'd never been so torn in his life. Between being a husband and being a Samaritan. That's why a lot of branches won't let husband and wife do duty together. We won't, now. We had a meeting about it; afterwards.

'Go *on*, Geoff. If she does anything silly, I'll never forgive myself. She might chuck herself in the river . . .'

They both knew. In our parts, the river or the drain is often the favourite way; rather than the usual overdose. The river seems to *call* to the locals, when life gets too much for them.

'Let's ring Tom again . . .'

She gave him a look that withered him and Tom together. In the silence that followed, they realized they were cut off from their duty-director, from *all* the directors, from *all* help. The most fatal thing, for Samaritans. They were poised on the verge of the ultimate sin; going it alone.

He made a despairing noise in his throat; reached for his coat and the car-keys. 'I'll do Yaxton Bridge. But I'll not do Moresby Abbey. It's a mile along the towpath in the dark. It'd take me an hour . . .'

He didn't wait for her dissent. He heard her lock the office door behind him. At least she'd be safe behind a locked door . . .

He never thought that telephones got past locked doors.

He made Yaxton Bridge in eight minutes flat, skidding and correcting his skids on the treacherous road. Lucky there wasn't much traffic about.

On his right, the River Ousam beckoned, flat, black, deep and still. A slight steam hung over the water, because it was just a little warmer than the air.

It was getting on for one, by the time he reached the lock. But there was still a light in one of the pair of lock-keeper's cottages. And he knew at a glance that this wasn't the place. No ice on the river; no fog. He hovered, unwilling to disturb the occupants. Maybe they were in bed, the light left on to discourage burglars.

But when he crept up the garden path, he heard the sound of the TV, a laugh, coughing. He knocked.

An elderly man's voice called through the door, 'Who's there?'

'Samaritans. I'm trying to find somebody's house. I'll push my card through your letter-box.'

He scrabbled frantically through his wallet in the dark. The door was opened. He passed through to a snug sitting-room, a roaring fire. The old man turned down the sound of the TV. The wife said he looked perished, and the Samaritans did such good work, turning out at all hours, even at Christmas. Then she went to make a cup of tea.

He asked the old man about ice, and fog, and a lock-keeper who lived alone with a lame wife. The old man shook his head. 'Couple who live next door's got three young kids . . .'

'Wife's not lame, is she?'

'Nay – a fine-lookin' lass wi' two grand legs on her . . .'

His wife, returning with the tea-tray, gave him a *very* old-fashioned look. Then she said, 'I've sort of got a memory of a lock-keeper wi' a lame wife – this was years ago, mind. Something not nice . . . but your memory goes, when you get old.'

'We worked the lock at Ousby Point on the coast, all our married lives,' said the old man apologetically. 'They just let us retire here, 'cos the cottage was goin' empty . . .'

Geoff scalded his mouth, drinking their tea, he was so frantic to get back. He did the journey in seven minutes; he was getting used to the skidding, by that time.

He parked the car outside the Sam. office, expecting her to hear his return and look out. But she didn't.

He knocked; he shouted to her through the door. No answer. Frantically he groped for his own key in the dark, and burst in.

She was sitting at the emergency phone, her face greyer than ever. Her eyes were far away, staring at the blank wall. They didn't swivel to greet him. He bent close to the phone in her hand and heard the same voice, the same cold hopeless tone, going on and on. It was sort of . . . hypnotic. He had to tear himself away, and grab a message pad. On it he scrawled, 'WHAT'S HAPPENING? WHERE IS SHE?'

He shoved it under Meg's nose. She didn't respond in any way at all. She seemed frozen, just listening. He pushed her shoulder, half angry, half frantic. But she was wooden, like a statue. Almost as if she was in a trance. In a wave of husbandly terror, he snatched the phone from her.

It immediately went dead.

He put it down, and shook Meg. For a moment she recognized him and smiled, sleepily. Then her face went rigid with fear.

'Her husband was in the house. He was just about to open the door where she was . . .'

'Did you find out where she was?'

'Moresby Abbey lock. She told me in the end. I got her confidence. Then *you* came and ruined it . . .'

She said it as if he was suddenly her enemy. An enemy, a fool, a bully, a murderer. Like all men. Then she said, 'I must go to her . . .'

'And leave the office unattended? That's *mad*.' He took off his coat with the car-keys, and hung it on the office door. He came back and looked at her again. She still seemed a bit odd, trance-like. But she smiled at him and said, 'Make me a quick cup of tea. I must go to the loo, before she rings again.'

Glad they were friends again, he went and put the kettle on. Stood impatiently waiting for it to boil, tapping his fingers on the sink-unit, trying to work out what they should do. He heard Meg's step in the hallway. Heard the toilet flush.

Then he heard a car start up outside.

His car.

He rushed out into the hall. The front door was swinging, letting in the snow. Where his car had been, there were only tyre-marks.

He was terrified now. Not for the woman. For Meg.

He rang Tom Brett, more frightened than any client Tom Brett had ever heard.

He told Tom what he knew.

'Moresby Locks,' said Tom. 'A lame woman. A murdering husband. Oh, my God. I'll be with you in five.'

'The exchange are putting emergency calls through to Jimmy Henry,' said Tom, peering through the whirling wet flakes that were clogging his windscreen-wipers. 'Do you know what way Meg was getting to Moresby Locks?'

'The only way,' said Geoff. 'Park at Wylop Bridge and walk a mile up the towpath.'

'There's a short cut. Down through the woods by the Abbey, and over the lock-gates. Not a lot of people know about it. I think we'll take that one. I want to get there before she does . . .'

'What the hell do you think's going on?'

'I've got an *idea*. But if I told you, you'd think I was out of my tiny shiny. So I won't. All I want is your Meg safe and dry, back in the Sam. office. And nothing in the log that head-quarters might see . . .'

He turned off the by-pass, into a narrow track where hawthorn bushes reached out thorny arms and scraped at the paintwork of the car. After a long while, he grunted with satisfaction, clapped on the brakes and said, 'Come on.'

They ran across the narrow wooden walkway that sat precariously on top of the lock-gates. The flakes of snow whirled at them, in the light of Tom's torch. Behind the gates, the water stacked up, black, smooth, slightly steaming because it was warmer than the air. In an evil way, it called to Geoff. So easy to slip in, let the icy arms embrace you, slip away . . .

Then they were over, on the towpath. They looked left, right, listened.

Footsteps, woman's footsteps, to the right. They ran that way.

Geoff saw Meg's walking back, in its white raincoat . . .

And beyond Meg, leading Meg, another back, another woman's back. The back of a woman who limped.

A woman with a dog. A little white dog . . .

For some reason, neither of them called out to Meg. Fear of disturbing a Samaritan relationship, perhaps. Fear of breaking up something that neither of them understood. After all, they could afford to be patient now. They had found Meg safe. They were closing up quietly on her, only ten yards away. No danger . . .

Then, in the light of Tom's torch, a break in the white-painted fence on the river side.

And the figure of the limping woman turned through the gap in the fence, and walked out over the still black waters of the river.

The Call

And like a sleepwalker, Meg turned to follow . . .

They caught her on the very brink. Each of them caught her
violently by one arm, like policemen arresting a criminal. Tom
cursed, as one of his feet slipped down the bank and into the
water. But he held on to them, as they all swayed on the
brink, and he only got one very wet foot.

'What the hell am I doing here?' asked Meg, as if waking from
a dream. 'She was talking to me. I'd got her confidence . . .'

'Did she tell you her name?'

'Agnes Todd.'

'Well,' said Tom, 'here's where Agnes Todd used to live.'

There were only low walls of stone, in the shape of a house.
With stretches of concrete and old broken tile in between.
There had been a phone, because there was still a telegraph
pole, with a broken junction-box from which two black wires
flapped like flags in the wind.

'Twenty-one years ago, Reg Todd kept this lock. His lame
wife Agnes lived with him. They didn't get on well – people
passing the cottage heard them quarrelling. Christmas Eve,
1964, he reported her missing to the police. She'd gone out for
a walk with the dog, and not come back. The police searched.
There was a bad fog down that night. They found a hole in the
railing, just about where we saw one; and a hole in the ice,
just glazing over. They found the dog's body next day; but
they didn't find her for a month, till the ice on the River
Ousam finally broke up.

'The police tried to make a case of it. Reg Todd *had* been
carrying on with a girl in the village. But there were no marks
of violence. In the end, she could have fallen, she could've
been pushed, or she could've jumped. So they let Reg Todd go;
and he left the district.'

There was a long silence. Then Geoff said, 'So you think . . .?'

'I think nowt,' said Tom Brett, suddenly very stubborn and
solid and Fenman. 'I think nowt, and that's all I *know*. Now
let's get your missus home.'

*

Nearly a year passed. In the November, after a short illness, Harry Lancaster died peacefully in his sleep. He had an enormous funeral. The church was full. Present Samaritans, past Samaritans from all over the country, more old clients than you could count, and even two of the top brass from Slough.

But it was not till everybody was leaving the house that Tom Brett stopped Geoff and Meg by the gate. More solid and Fenman than ever.

'I had a long chat wi' Harry,' he said, 'after he knew he was goin'. He told me. About Agnes Todd. She had rung him up on Christmas Eve. Every Christmas Eve for twenty years . . .'

'Did he know she was a . . .?' Geoff still couldn't say it.

'Oh, aye. No flies on Harry. The second year – while he was still director – he persuaded the GPO to get an engineer to trace the number. How he managed to get them to do it on Christmas Eve, God only knows. But he had a way with him, Harry, in his day.'

'And . . .'

'The GPO were baffled. It was the old number of the lock-cottage all right. But the lock-cottage was demolished a year after the . . . whatever it was. Nobody would live there, afterwards. All the GPO found was a broken junction-box and wires trailin'. Just like we saw that night.'

'So he talked to her all those years . . . knowing?'

'Aye, but he wouldn't let anybody else do Christmas Eve. She was lonely, but he knew she was dangerous. Lonely an' dangerous. She wanted company.'

Meg shuddered. 'How could he bear it?'

'He was a Samaritan . . .'

'Why didn't he tell anybody?'

'Who'd have believed him?'

There were half a dozen of us in the office this Christmas Eve. Tom Brett, Maureen, Meg and Geoff, me. All waiting for . . .

It never came. Nobody called at all.

'Do you think?' asked Maureen, with an attempt at a smile,

her hand to her throat in a nervous gesture, in the weak light of dawn.

'Aye,' said Tom Brett. 'I think we've heard the last of her. Mebbe Harry took her with him. Or came back for her. Harry was like that. The best Samaritan I ever knew.'

His voice went funny on the last two words, and there was a shine on those stolid Fenman eyes. He said, 'I'll be off then.' And was gone.

The Red House Clock

I was born into poverty. Poverty of mind.

My father taught himself to read after he married. By slowly deciphering the tombstones in the churchyard in his dinner-hour. He would sit with a hunk of bread and cheese in one hand, slowly tracing the carved letters with the other. Because the tombstones were of men he'd known, he managed in the end. Well enough to print a short note, or read the *Daily Sketch*.

He did it out of desperation. Because he'd married the schoolmaster's daughter, and my mother's unspoken contempt grieved him.

My mother married beneath her. She married a farm-labourer for his looks. For long, my father was the handsomest man in the village, with his tall upright figure, jet-black hair and pale blue eyes. She made a bad mistake. He was not only the handsomest, he was the hardest. In a village of hard men.

I must make this clear. He wasn't a cruel man. Not a sadist. Nor a drunkard that beat his wife, like some. But he was unforgiving, like the flint the ploughs turned up in the fields of Suffolk.

They said my mother's father died of shame at the marriage. Leaving them his house and furniture, the luxury of tapped cold water, and his books. It was as well he did, for we would have lived poorly on what a cowman earned, in the 1920s. My father was lucky to have a job at all. Lots of farm-labourers were idle. Empire Preference, New Zealand lamb, New Zealand cheese and butter, Australian wool saw to that. They were cheaper, and at home the farms were left to rot. My father

95

survived because he was a good cowman. And besides, he was good at mending things that seemed beyond repair; worn-out harness, buckets with holes in them, the village pump.

So we lived in our genteel poverty. Everything in the house was so polished and dusted you could see your face in it. But nothing changed. Nothing new was bought. My father and I walked round in our stockinged feet, for fear of wearing out the carpets.

At five, I went to school. Learnt to read quickly, as my mother had.

The first time I brought home a book to read, my father threw it out of the window into the forest of bean-plants and marigolds that was our garden. My poor mother ran out to rescue it, cleaned the wet soil off it with a look of horror on her face. It went back to school the following day cleaner and more highly polished than it had ever been. But I never dared bring home another.

Two weeks later, my grandfather's books were sold to the dealer in the village. My father got five pounds for them; he spent the money on a gift for my mother. A second-hand hen-cree and a dozen Rhode Island Red pullets. They laid abundantly. (Just as well for them, or my father would've wrung their necks.) We were glad of the eggs, and the little money they brought in, which my mother spent mainly, I think, on furniture polish. But she never forgave him for what he'd done, though only the tightness of her lips whenever he came home told me so.

Even the *Daily Sketch* was denied me, as I grew older. If I was caught with it, I was clouted and sent outside to play 'in God's good fresh air'. Each edition was carried off to the old shed where my father mended things. Only to reappear when a fire was being lit; or wrapped round some broad beans to be taken to the Red House, where the produce of my father's large garden was famous. Even my mother dared not ask to read it. Reading was for idle dreamers. The only thing that mattered was what a man could do with his hands.

I read everything I could lay my hands on at school. But

there was no library in a village school in those days. Enough that farm-labourers' children could read and write at all, before they went into service at the big house, or to work on the land.

My mind starved. Or would have starved, but for Tip. Tip was the dealer my father sold my grandfather's books to. He was often at our house, for a cup of tea. But only in the evenings, of course, when my father was home.

For some reason, the one soft spot in my father's heart was kept for Tip. Yet they couldn't have been more opposite. Where my father was tall, Tip was little. Where my father was brown and muscular from the fields, Tip was pale and plump. Where my father strode, Tip limped. Where my father was handsome, Tip was as ugly as a frog with his gold-rimmed spectacles and balding head. And where my father was silent, but for grunts, Tip could talk the hind leg off a donkey, as my father said. But he was always welcome. What he saw in us, I have long wondered. Perhaps he was sweet on my mother. Perhaps she was a little sweet on him. Though she never spoke, getting on with her ironing while Tip and my father sat on rockers each side of the kitchen fire, she often smiled at his stories. Secretly, down towards the smell of hot cotton on the ironing board.

And what stories they were! Tip and my father had both been in the Great War, and both had been wounded. But whereas my father had somehow survived the Battle of the Somme, Tip had served in Egypt and the Far East. He was full of yarns of Egyptian mummies and bazaars, and Chinese pirates in their junks. How much of his stories was just made up, none of us had any way of knowing. But he fed my young soul.

It was natural that as I grew older, I should be drawn to Tip's shop. For I will say this for my father; he would let neither my mother nor I go out stone-picking for a pound a cartful. The stones were picked from the fields, and used to mend the farm-roads.

Most farm-labourers' wives were expected to do it; were even glad to do it. But my father said if a man could not support a wife and family without their aid. he was not fit to be called a man. So I had plenty of spare time, and I spent it with Tip.

He was a kind of dealer you don't get today. Bluntly, he auctioned off the belongings of the dead. And of people who were desperately emigrating to Australia or Canada, hoping to change their luck. And of people who went bankrupt (but I'll come to that later). But mainly, the furniture and possessions of the dead who had no relatives. The undertaker came for the body, and Tip dealt with the rest. Usually by a house sale; held in the house the Saturday morning after the funeral. Half the neighbourhood turned up for them; they were as good as a party; he made people laugh. Not in a nasty city-slicker way, but with sympathy.

'How much for George's old frying-pan,' he'd say, 'that's cooked many a borrowed egg!' And everyone would laugh, remembering George's little ways. Or, 'How about Miss Letty's wedding-dress? She died at eighty, but she never gave up hoping!' It was all a bit like the funeral tea; remembering the deceased and the funny things that had once happened to them. Tip was well-liked, all round the village, though he'd only lived there since the War, and lived in Staffordshire as a young lad.

Of course, there was the other side to the laughter. The night before the sale, when he went up to the dead person's house, to sort and label the stuff into lots. He often took me with him, even when I was only eleven or twelve. It was not that he was *scared*; but he felt things deeply. And so did I. Walking into a house after a funeral is like walking into a dead person's life. The cups and plates from the funeral tea, sometimes washed-up in the sink, and sometimes just left lying, all crumbs. The chair the dead person had sat in by the fire; still showing the hollows left by their body. Their wilting pot-plants, or dying flowers in vases. The clocks they had wound up still ticking. The bundles of staring brown photographs that fell out of cupboards; the darned vests and socks.

'The secrets of all hearts shall be revealed,' Tip used to say. 'The secrets of all hearts.'

And sometimes I thought you could feel the person still there, watching us; watching to see what we did with their life. Some felt happy, like Granny Burscombe, with her Bible open for its daily reading, at Matthew 13, and a bundle of receipts from the cripples' home, for the half-crowns she'd sent them every month for thirty years.

'She had a soul like a bird,' said Tip, 'these last few weeks. A joyous bird waiting to fly out of her earthly cage and up to her Maker.'

Or the poor empty hovel of Charlie Fairbrother, who had played the piano round the village pubs for thirty years, for the drinks people gave him; and lived on very little else. We found his music diploma, and a faded photograph of him with his massed choirboys, standing at the door of some great church.

'What a waste of a life,' said Tip. 'There was a Great Fall there, somewhere. But he wasn't unhappy in the end. Not really unhappy. He lived the way he wanted.'

But sometimes the dead person felt angry; as if they *hadn't* lived the way they'd wanted. We found things that Tip read and whistled over, and quickly burnt in the grate. 'We don't want to cause trouble, do we, lad?'

He trusted me to keep my mouth shut. And I never let him down. But the fascination of the job grew on me. The things of the dead became my books; my knowledge was all inside my head, where my father could not reach it.

There were other perks, too. I helped Tip a lot; enough to be paid a wage. But money was short then; Tip only managed to get by, like all the rest of us. So he let me take things from the houses that weren't worth selling. Hanks of old wire. Collections of old string. (My God, how we collected knotted old string in those days. My mother had an apple-crate full of it, all colours and thicknesses.) Part-used tins of boot-polish; part-used bottles of Brasso. At first, I took these things home for my mother. But she refused them with a slight shudder, and said I didn't know where they'd been. Then I understood she feared the dead. Which seemed strange to me; for I had no fear of them at all. And I stored all these things in a tea-chest in the corner of my bedroom. It became a safe place to hide things, for I knew my mother would never touch it.

Tip kept things, too. Things that didn't fetch enough in the auctions, he would buy himself. And then they would appear in the window of his shop, and gather dust from year to year. That was how I got my first bicycle. I had yearned over it for months, poor rusted, tyreless thing, until he gave it to me for a Christmas present. My father helped me get it back to working order in his workshop. That was the closest we ever got, that world of prising rusted cogs apart, and soaking them in oil and paraffin, and sorting through the bunches of part-worn tyres that festooned the ceiling of Tip's shop like dusty black tropical fruit. I think my father sensed in me a desire to mend, a cleverness at mending, that was the first thing he ever approved of. Almost the only thing about me he ever approved of. We were in the world of things, not the world of books, and he did not mind my cleverness at all.

After that, the desire to mend and renew seized me. It seemed to me that dead men's things had a right to life, to live again. They became, if you like, my pets. You will ask, did I never as a child have any pets? My mother had a yellow canary, that sang beautifully, to her delight, on sunlit mornings. Though my father grumbled often about the cost of seed for it, and she fed it mainly on groundsel and rat's tails and other seeding plants that she gathered in the fields and garden. But I soon learnt the foolishness of loving animals. I tried loving our family pig when I was very little; till the day I heard it squealing when my father cut its throat. I learnt that kittens were quickly drowned, and that sheep-dogs too old to work were shot. Oh, yes, I learnt the hard way not to love animals.

But that old brass alarm-clock in Tip's window ... Black with verdigris and never a tick to be got out of it, no matter how hard people shook it. I handled it so often that, with a sigh of exasperation, Tip finally gave it me to get some peace.

I ran home with it. That night, my father helped me to turn

the screws that held it together. (Oh, the trained sinewy power of his wrists.) We found, to our mutual delight, that the works were only thick with grey fluff. It had wakened an old couple called Johnson all their married lives, and afterwards, every morning, the wife must have made her bed, tossing the blankets with vigour, filling the air with grey particles of wool that crept into the crevices of the clock and finally choked it. My father left the works soaking for an hour in a battered bucket of paraffin, then rinsed them vigorously, and they came up in his hand gleaming and burst into ticking life. It was like the Resurrection.

I kept the brass case soaking for a week in a bowl of vinegar (a nearly full pint bottle left behind by Mrs Springs, who loved vinegar all her life) and then polished it with the Brasso Mr Parsons had once used to clean his candlesticks, and we put it back together, gleaming and ticking and ringing like new. And I put it in Tip's window, with a price-tag of two shillings, and old Simmins who had sharp eyes bought it on the second day, and it gave him good service, and I never passed him standing at his garden gate without he said, 'Your clock's still agoing a treat, boy!'

It was then that I realized where old Tip was going wrong. He had a good eye for a bargain. He had a good eye for faults and flaws in anything. I have known him stand for twenty minutes just holding a thing lovingly and looking at it close, as if he was a balding, short-sighted squirrel. He had an eye for beauty. Looking back now, I realize that the grease-blackened chair he sat in at the shop every day was a priceless Chippendale. That he kept his unpaid bills behind a Staffordshire 'Nelson' that would fetch several hundred pounds at modern prices. He dwelt in beauty, did Tip.

But he never cleaned or polished or even dusted anything. Let alone mended it. He was always a scruffy little beggar . . .

Now I'd say, 'Let me have a go at it, Tip!' And he'd smile and nod, and I'd bear the object away home and use up all my love and oil, Brasso and shoe-polish on it, and bring it back gleaming. And it would sell straightaway. Off to a new life. I saved things from decay as the Salvation Army saved souls from hell. With the same fire in my belly.

But my great love was clocks. Nothing lives like a clock. Nothing can be your friend on a lonely dark evening like a clock. Its tick greets you, as you walk in through your door. Its chime reminds you when it's time to make your supper. Each has a personality. American clocks limp their way through the world like a weary man. German clocks are exact and precise. When I was all het-up, the slow tick of an English long-case would soothe me. When I was drear, French clocks would brisk me up with their sharp tick and bright 'ting'.

I loved nothing better than to discover a clock in a house we were selling-up. In some cupboard, long-abandoned. Thick with cobwebs as a haunted house; blistered all down one side by the sun; stained white with the creeping blight of damp. Clocks like little houses, little haunted churches, little ruined black temples, from which all life had gone and only memory remained. And I would say, like Jesus said of the widow's son, 'He is not dead, but sleepeth.' And set to work.

Of course, the village people, and even I myself, had no idea of antiques in those days. When I remember the clocks I bought off Tip for a shilling, and sold again for five, I could weep now. But people just needed a good clock to tell the time by. Even in the 1930s, most village people had no radio to keep time by. People began calling at the shop, asking if the boy had a good sound clock to sell.

On my fourteenth birthday, I left school. No waiting till the end of the summer term. I was suddenly a man, with my living to make. There had been talk of my going on the farm where my father worked, for a pound a week wages. The farmer offered, and my father saw it as a great favour. God knows what might have happened to me, if I'd gone. I might be shovelling cow-muck with an aching back yet.

But Tip, bless him, asked for me. Offering the same wage. And my father, comforting himself that there was no book-learning involved, let me go to him. He admired my mending of things by then; said I was as good as he was. I think he almost envied me my new job, when his back was bad after harvest.

Of course, once I was Tip's employee, he could no longer protect me from the unpleasant side of the job. It wasn't selling-up the goods of those who were emigrating to Canada and Australia I minded. They were sad occasions, for people were leaving their whole families behind for ever. But Tip could cheer even those up.

'Fine pair of wellies – lots of wear in them yet. Tommy won't need those when he's chasing kangaroos in the Outback!'

And everyone would laugh, and cough up what they could.

No. It was the bankruptcy sales. I suppose bankruptcy isn't so bad now. You think of posh businessmen selling up their business from the comfort of the bungalow they're allowed to keep, before they start making their fortune again.

But ours were different. It meant a family losing everything they had. Wife and kids going into the workhouse, while the husband set off tramping round England to look for work which wasn't there.

And we only had one cause of bankruptcy. A Scotsman called MacClintock. That most hated of men, a moneylender. He lived next door to us. But my mother and father never mentioned him by name. He was always 'him next door' with an angry jerk of the head. They never spoke to him. Nobody in the village ever spoke to him.

I used to watch him with fascinated horror, as he got into his black Austin Ten every morning, to drive to his pawnshops in Ipswich. A thin pale man, with Brylcreemed hair. My mother said you could tell he was dishonest, because his eyes were too close together. (I used to stare at myself in the mirror in my bedroom, to make sure that my eyes weren't too close together.) He had the prim correctness of a bank clerk; but there was a darkness about him, a sense of secrets, like you get with some undertakers. I don't know why he chose to live in our village; except that the house he lived in had come to him from a man he'd made bankrupt.

Of course, he had no interest in the village people. He was after bigger fish than us. But he was there, you see. And every so often, somebody in the village would get so desperate for money, they'd go to him, in spite of all the warnings. Maybe to get the money to give their old dad a proper funeral. Or for medical treatment for a sick child. And once they were in his clutches, they'd never get out. It was just a matter of time before his bailiffs were removing their furniture to sell.

It was the interest he charged, see. Suppose he loaned somebody five pounds. He'd only give them four – the other pound would be the first month's interest. And a pound interest every month after that. And if they couldn't pay, he'd offer to lend them more . . . And he ate up our little fish just as hungrily as the big fish in Ipswich.

Tip didn't like doing business with him. But business was business. And money was short.

And so we'd end up auctioning children's dolls and prams, and mens' medals, that they'd won in the War. I had to hold the things up, and I felt filthy afterwards. Nobody in the village came to those sales, there weren't any jokes to cheer you on. But plenty of other people did come. MacClintock's horrible little dealer-mates from all the towns and villages around. A pack of shabby ill-tempered men who squabbled over the lots like vultures over a carcase, Tip said, and having been out East, he should know.

It was broad bean time, August, when the trouble at the Red House started. The first I heard of it was my father complaining that they hadn't sent down for any of his broad beans this year. He was proud of selling them his broad beans. And besides, every sixpence counted. And Dad liked his little chats with the Major; because they'd both been through the War in France.

'They must've forgotten,' he said. 'I've a mind to walk up with some, on the off-chance.'

'Don't,' said my mother. 'There's something funny going on. They've given the cook her notice. No trouble, either. People reckon they can't afford to keep her.'

'That's daft,' said my father. 'Keeping a maid and letting the cook go.'

'Little you know,' said my mother. 'What do you men talk about? Maid got her notice three months ago.'

'Come to think of it, I haven't seen the Major's car round for a bit. Last time I saw him, he was pushing Miss Gwendoline in her wheelchair. I thought it was funny at the time . . .'

'It's awful,' said my mother. 'It doesn't bear thinking of. Miss Gwendoline's getting worse, and now with all the servants going, he'll be having to see to her all by himself . . .'

It was a terrible shock for me. The Major was the nearest thing we had to a Squire in the village. His family had lived in the Red House for a hundred years. Not that it was a very big house. My mother, who'd had friends in service there, said it only had six bedrooms. But that seemed big to me then.

And the Major was a sort of hero of mine, though I would never have dared to speak to him. He had won the MC in the War, for knocking out a German machine-gun post that was pinning down his company on the Hindenburg Line. He often saved people from MacClintock, with a little money and a lot of advice. I used to watch him stumping round the village on his wounded leg, chewing his grey moustache as if to hide the pain, and whistling softly, almost under his breath, a little tune that nobody in the village had ever heard before. I mean, everybody whistled in those days, rent-collectors and butcher's boys delivering. But they whistled songs from the West End shows. And nobody could put a name to the Major's song. Maybe he picked it up overseas in the War . . .

And Miss Gwendoline I loved from a distance. Even in her wheelchair, she was such a beautiful lady, with huge grey eyes and long slender hands, and a lovely pale smile for everybody. She came to the village school to give out the prizes. And always opened the Church Fete and Flower Show. The village men would jostle for the privilege of lifting her and her chair on to the platform, ever so gently.

We knew the family had fallen on hard times. They'd had to sell off the farms they owned before the War, and not got much for them. But they still gave to all the good causes; nobody ever asked in vain. They were one of the pillars of my young universe, and when they began to fall, the world never seemed quite the same again to me.

It was nearly the following Easter – Maundy Thursday – when the trouble at the Big House ended. Both Tip and I had been to Miss Gwendoline's funeral that morning; me in my first grown-up suit with long trousers, and Tip in a suit so shiny with age you could almost see your face in it. Tip had gone out to the pub at lunchtime, and not come back by three o'clock. That wasn't like him – he wasn't a great drinker. But I supposed he was drowning his sorrow over Miss Gwendoline, like so many of the village men. And I had a good fire roaring up our stove, and was fiddling with an old clock that refused to chime – an American Gilbert I think it was.

When he finally came in, he just stood, with his hands on the counter. He stood so long silent, I thought he was ill, and got up to him with a rush. I helped him into his chair and he said, 'The Major's dead an' all, Billy.'

'Dead?'

'Hanged hisself in the scullery at the Red House. Tommy Hargreaves was worried about him and went up to see he was all right, and found him hanging. In the scullery.'

'But . . . why?'

'He left a note – apologizing to the one that found him – and saying that MacClintock had taken him for every penny he had. MacClintock's got everything – the house, the land, the furniture.'

'But . . . how?'

'Medical bills for Miss Gwendoline, they reckon. Best o' the Harley Street specialists, and they cost money. MacClintock was putting in the bailiffs, day after the funeral.'

We were both silent a long time. I was used to life being hard in our village. But I had never dreamt there could be such evil in the world.

Then Tip said, 'I saw MacClintock in the village on the way

home. Bold as brass, as if nothing had happened. The wicked shall flourish as the green bay tree. He wants me to auction off the Major's stuff – week come Saturday.'

'You'll not do it?'

He sighed. 'I've got to, Billy. I've got to see the stuff's handled with respect. For the Major and Miss Gwendoline's sake. You don't want them mauling her stuff about, do you? And mebbe there's things people shouldn't see. It's the least I can do for the Major . . . I'll not ask you to come with me, Billy. It's too much to ask a young lad.'

I looked at him then, sitting little and fat and defeated in his chair. And I loved him, as I'd never loved my father, or even my mother. He was the most decent, feeling little soul I ever knew.

'I'll come with you, Tip,' I said. 'It's not a job for one feller on his own.'

'God bless you, son,' he said, and gripped my hand tight.

Well, we did it. Together. I soon saw what Tip meant, about taking care of the Major. There was a diary, full of despair he'd never shown in public. There was his MC, which Tip put in his pocket, to send to his old regiment. There were photographs; of Miss Gwendoline, when she was young and well and laughing; of another beautiful lady, who must have been her mother. Signed 'To my beloved husband'. Family letters. Photographs of dogs he had loved. Tip put them all into an old Gladstone bag, to be burnt, or sent to those who cared.

I'm afraid I kept glancing towards the dreadful scullery, where it had happened. Till in the end Tip took me by the hand, and led me straight into it. Made me look at the rusty iron hook in the ceiling.

'He was a good man,' said Tip, with a quaver in his voice. 'He was a good man who looked after people in this village, the best he could. Who never did any harm to no one. Life was very cruel to him, Billy. Took away his wife, his daughter, his money, his house. But he wouldn't be a burden to anyone. They couldn't take away his pride. God bless you, Major, wherever you are. Well done, old lad.'

I cried then; and it must have done me good. Because I was never afraid of the Major, or that scullery, or that whole house again.

We got on with labelling the stuff for auction. There wasn't much left. You could see the big dark patches on the wallpaper, where family portraits and such had once hung. Marks on the carpet, where furniture had once stood. Tip said the Major had had some lovely stuff, especially just after the War, before his wife died. 'A picture, the house was, then. But all gone to pay the doctor's bills, Billy. Bit by bit. Till he only had MacClintock left to turn to. May he rot in hell.'

All that was left were the things in two bedrooms, a couch Miss Gwendoline had lain on and, on the marble mantelpiece . . .

A great clock. The greatest clock I had ever seen. I almost tiptoed up to it, it was so great.

It was in mahogany, in the shape of a castle, nearly two feet high. There were turrets and spires and windows and a door under the clock-face, with its Gothic numerals painted on little shields made of ivory. The intricate hands were of gilded brass. It was stopped, of course. Long stopped from the look of it. Thick with dust and cobwebs, blistered down one side by the sun, and with white streaks from damp. A ruin of a great clock. A haunted castle of a clock. I lifted a trembling finger to move the minute hand round to twelve.

The clock stirred to life, with a deep-down ghostly whirring. And then it struck; a great gong-like sound that echoed through the whole house. Nine, it struck, so loud I wanted to stop it, but couldn't. And then, the doors at the bottom, below the great dial, flicked open one by one, and wooden trumpeters emerged with stiff jerks, and raised jerky trumpets to their carved lips. And inside the clock, trumpets sounded; a tune. Slow, jerky, stopping in the middle. But a tune none the less.

'That's the Major's tune,' said Tip, awed. 'The one he used to whistle round the village. Musta been a German tune. The Major musta brought the clock back from Germany, after the War.'

The tune began again; then ground to a jerky halt and died. It was as if the Major had died again.

'Let's get on with the labelling,' said Tip.

Tip dropped me at home. He leaned across and shouted through the old van's window, 'Take four days off, Billy. I'm not opening the shop, Saturday. Have a good rest, son. You done well. Thanks a lot.'

As he drove away, I knew he was going to get drunker than he'd ever been in his life.

It was only when I walked through our kitchen door that I felt something in my pocket, banging against my leg.

I'd forgotten to give him the keys to the Red House back.

I'll not ask you to believe the rest. But I'll tell it to you just the same. I dreamt that night that the Major came back to see me. He had a red groove round his neck, where the rope had marked him, but he smiled at me pleasantly. In every way, he was his same old self.

'Mend my clock, laddo,' he said. 'It's all that's left of me now. And I've still got a job I want to do.' Then he went stumping off, in his old way, with a casual wave of the hand. He was so nice and ordinary, I didn't even wake up in a cold sweat. I slept well, and woke up feeling fine.

That was Good Friday. I left home as if I was going to the shop. My mother was a bit put out, as she wanted me to go to church with her on Good Friday as usual. People went to church on Good Friday in those days; nearly all the village shops stayed closed. But I said Tip had a big job he wanted doing. And I gathered together all my bottles of oil and tins of polish and bits and pieces in an old brown-paper carrier-bag and took them as well.

I must say, I suffered a few tremors, as I opened the front door on that silent house. But it was all right. The sun was shining in through the great high sash windows, lighting up the walls and ceilings. Even all faded, they were gentle and beautiful. I suppose it sounds daft, but I felt all the love there'd been in that house, over all the years. And on the sitting-room's faded Persian carpet, I saw a square of white, face down. It was a photo of Miss Gwendoline, when she was young and well and happy. I suppose Tip must have dropped it, out of his bag. But I set her on the old table, beside the clock, which I lifted down carefully from the mantelpiece. And she smiled up at me, as I set to work. It was going to be OK. I was doing what the Major wanted; I was doing what she wanted. I have never felt so calm in my life. Calm, and sunshine. I have never felt happier, those four days.

For four days it took me. The clock was very intricate; the hardest I'd ever tried. I should have despaired often; but something bore me up. I eased and I oiled. And by the end of the third day, it ticked and chimed and blew on its tiny bellows that made the trumpet noise, faultlessly. The noise filled the whole house, and made it glad, with the Major's old tune. I left it ticking that night, and I found it still ticking on the fourth morning.

So that last day, I spent polishing. The wood came up like new, and the brass bezel and little brass decorations shone almost like silver. And so I left it, glowing like a jewel in that shabby faded house. It lived. And while it lived, there was something of the Major and Miss Gwendoline left in the world. It would find its way to someone who loved it; someone who it would keep safe.

But on the morning of the auction, it was gone. There was only the dark place on the wall above the mantelpiece, where it had been.

'Where's the clock?' I hissed at Tip.

'MacClintock,' he hissed back. 'He took one look at it, and took it for hisself. Said it was the only decent thing left in the house and swore he'd have it. Reckoned the Major had cheated him, selling off the last of his pictures. He put the clock in his car and drove straight home. I doubt we'll see him again today.'

It was as well we didn't. I felt like murdering MacClintock

with my bare hands, small though I was, and him a grown man. I felt that I'd brought the Major back to life, only to deliver him back into prison, at the hands of his worst enemy.

I was still lying awake in bed that night, writhing with rage, when I heard the sound from next door. (My bedroom window faced MacClintock's house, across the narrow alleyway between.)

The clock was chiming. Nine, ten, eleven, twelve, thirteen, on and on. And the trumpets blowing the Major's tune fit to wake the whole village. Fit to wake the dead.

And then a crash, at last. And silence.

Late the next day, Tubby Pinns the gaffer of our council dustmen came into the shop. He was quite useful to us, Tubby. And we were quite useful to him. Sometimes people put the most amazing things in their dustbins, like bundles of brass stair-rods, or encyclopaedias, or books about the Great War in very good condition. And of course, Tubby came round to us, and flogged them for a bob, to share among the lads.

That day, he came in with his arms full of something that looked like a small suitcase, with funny knobs on top.

It wasn't till he put it down that I saw it was the Major's clock. He'd found it chucked down in the back lane by MacClintock's dustbin, with other rubbish.

It had taken a battering. The case was split from top to bottom, as if someone had struck it a dreadful blow. The glass of the dial was smashed too, and the hands bent.

'Any use to you? I'll take a bob for it. I know you like clocks.'

Tip gave him a bob out of his waistcoat pocket, and he went. I hurried across to the clock, like a mother to a hurt child. It was not as bad as I feared. The case was split; but it had split down the glued joints. The old glue had given way instead of the wood, and that had saved it. The brass bezel was bent, the knobs had fallen off (Tubby had produced a lot from the pockets of his faded blue jacket). But it was all there. I could repair it. I heaved a sigh of relief.

'The bastard,' said Tip. 'The rotten Scottish bastard. How low can you get? Taking it home just to break it like that. He must have really *hated* the Major.'

Somehow, even then, I didn't think it was quite like that. But I didn't say anything to him. I was too busy fussing over the clock. Working out how to get it back and going again. So that the Major and Miss Gwendoline could go on living.

I got it back and going perfectly in exactly a week. Polished off the white spots where it had been rained on, overnight, beside the dustbins. I put it in Tip's shop window, where everyone could see it and admire it, and hear it strike and trumpet. Somehow, my latest repairs seemed to have strengthened it. It now chimed and blew so loud, it seemed as loud as the church clock, echoing from one end of our little village street to the other. Even lying in bed at night, I'd hear it faintly, and know that all was well with it.

Two days later, I came back from getting my dinner to find Tip and MacClintock both in the shop going hammer and tongs. Tip was shouting, 'I'll not sell it to you, you Scottish loonie. You just want to break it again, don't you? Like you broke it before? Well, you're not going to get the chance.'

'Just name your price,' said MacClintock, in a low strained voice. 'How much do you want? Fifty? A hundred?'

I heard Tip gasp. A hundred pounds was a year's wages for a farm-labourer in those days. But still he shook his head.

'It's a fine clock. The lad's slaved over it. I'll *not* do that to him!'

'Two hundred,' yelled MacClintock. 'Two hundred, ye stupid little loon.' He seized Tip's lapels with both his hands.

That was a mistake.

'Take your hands off me,' said Tip in a hating, icy voice. 'I'll not sell that clock to you for any amount.'

'Four hundred,' said MacClintock, letting go of him.

I saw Tip hesitate. He was the dearest man under the sun; but he was also a dealer. And four hundred pounds was the price of a good farmhouse, then.

MacClintock saw the hesitation too. 'Five hundred,' he said, snatching out his wallet so it dropped on the floor and white banknotes spilled out. It is terrible the effect the sight of banknotes has on people. Even people as good as Tip.

'Done,' he said, sharp and keen, just thinking about the money.

MacClintock counted out the notes into Tip's silent hand; twice one fell on the floor. Then he snatched up the clock with a terrible jangle, and was gone, clutching it to his chest.

'Tip!' I screamed. '*Tip!*'

He came out of his money-daze, and his face was all concern for me. 'Lad, lad, don't fret. I'll give you half. It'll set you up for life . . .'

But I didn't stop to listen. I ran out after MacClintock. Even though it was raining, I didn't stop for my coat. I saw MacClintock's car vanishing up the street. He didn't turn for home, he turned the other way.

I ran after him; I ran and ran, thinking only of the clock and the Major and Miss Gwendoline. I ran till my lungs felt they were bursting, till I got a stitch in my side. And still I staggered on. Even though I knew it was hopeless.

I caught up with him at Tom Pickering's little garage at the far end of the village. Tom only had one petrol-pump in those days, and he had just finished filling a gallon can of petrol. He gave it to MacClintock, and MacClintock gave him money and got back into his car with the full can.

I knew then that he was going to burn the clock, after he'd smashed it. He saw me leaning exhausted against the garage fence as he passed, and he laughed at me, and I saw the clock through the car window for the last time . . .

I nearly gave up. I could run no further. And MacClintock's house was half a mile away. And yet I could not give up. Something wouldn't let me. I ran and walked, ran and walked, as the Boy Scouts taught you then.

By the time I got home, and peeped over our garden fence, into the back lane, he had smashed the clock to a pile of smithereens, and was just pouring the petrol over it. He got a match out of his pocket, lit it, and threw it on the broken pile, and it went up whoomf with a blue flame.

And then the heavens really opened. Whole rods of rain. Drenching rain. How different all our lives would have been since, if the heavens had not opened up then. How different everything would have been . . .

MacClintock gave a glance at the burning pile, to make sure it was still alight, then ran indoors, his grey raincoat turning black at the shoulders with the rain.

And I ran out into the lane. Kicked the burning pile apart. Beat out the flames with the cap snatched from my head, with my bare hands, not even feeling the pain till afterwards, though my mother had to dress my blisters that night before bed. The rain helped a lot . . .

The back of the clock was still intact. It formed a shallow broken box, and into it, weeping, I piled all the broken fragments. Then ran into my father's shed with it.

My father was there, mending a mousetrap. They sent farmhands home when it rained, in those days.

I said to him, 'MacClintock's smashed the clock again!'

And my father said, picking up odd bits and looking at them hopelessly, 'He's really done it this time. The feller's *bonkers*. That clock was worth *real* money.'

'I'll take it up to my bedroom,' I said, trying hard not to cry in front of him. It didn't do you any good to cry in front of my father; he called it going on like a wet girl.

I carried it up. My mother complained about having such rubbish in the house, but I wasn't in any mood to heed her. Alone in my bedroom, I wept buckets again, for the sheer hopelessness of life.

But then . . . the wreckage seemed to call to me. Eyes still full of tears, I picked up the bottom half of a smashed pinnacle. Of course, then I had to find the other half, and saw by the way it had snapped, with the grain, that the two halves could be glued together again. I reached for the glue; and the glue dried my tears. *Bits* of the clock could still be saved. I could keep the bits to remember the Major by.

At some point, MacClintock must have come back to check his wreckage. I heard him and my father shouting at each other across the garden wall. My father was at his most bloody-minded. I think he had always hated MacClintock, for what he'd done to the village people. He'd often threatened to break his neck. I think he hated him much more, after the Major died. And now he despised him for breaking the clock and wasting his own money. My father had a feeling for objects, and for money, that he never had for living things.

Anyway, over a long weary time MacClintock feverishly demanded his bits back, and my father told him to get lost. My father called him a Scots loonie. MacClintock threatened to send for the police, and my father offered to knock MacClintock's teeth down his throat. They both knew the village bobby hated MacClintock as much as everybody else. In the end, MacClintock shut up and went away.

And then Tip turned up, and I was summoned downstairs. Tip was waving white five-pound notes about, and having a terrible fit of conscience about the whole thing. He insisted on giving me half, and my mother took it from him to put in the savings bank for me. My father looked dazed at the sight of all that money, but he made no objection. Hard man he might have been, but too proud to steal off his only son . . .

After Tip had gone, I went back upstairs. Oddly enough, the money made no difference. Didn't cheer me up at all, though my mother said I could have five pounds to buy a brand new bike. I just got on with rescuing tiny bits of the clock and fitting them together, like I was crazy too.

And then my father came in, and saw what I was doing. He didn't call me a fool. He just squatted down on his haunches, and began picking up bits as well. After a long time, he said grimly, 'Reckon we can mend it. It'll take months, though.'

I really loved him then.

It takes a lot to stop a young lad from loving.

Even my indefatigable father despaired many times. Repairing the wooden case was easy enough, just tedious. Again, it was the glued joints mainly that had given way, and saved the wood. He left that to me, and in the end, I managed it. Close-to, the mended splits showed, under however many layers of polish I put on it, so it looked a bit like a jigsaw puzzle. But from a distance of four feet, it looked its old self. I straightened the enamelled face, and repainted the places where the enamel had chipped. The bezel and glass were a total write-off, but my father scoured the junk-shops till he found an exact replacement from another German clock lying without works. I spent a week straightening the hands millimetre by millimetre, with a tiny pair of pliers.

Meanwhile, my father had to sort out the scattered and twisted cogs, like an archaeologist. Even when he got each straightened and in its right place, the thing wouldn't go. He had to hand it over to the clockmaker in Wivenby, and it cost him a whole week's wages. It was then I began to wonder at the extremity of his love for me.

But when that was done, and the clock ticked and struck and chimed again, and my father had cut up my mother's best pair of kid-gloves to make anew the little bellows that sounded the trumpet-noises, we put it together one evening . . . And it worked. It struck and chimed and blew the old tune, somehow more loudly than ever.

I hugged him, and thanked him, and we set it up on a table in my room. He gave a strange grin, and said, 'Now let's wait and see!'

I didn't know what he was talking about. But I hadn't all that long to wait. We'd scarcely sat down to a celebration supper of sausages when there came a thunderous knocking at the door.

MacClintock burst into the room, pushing my mother aside so she fell against the wall. His eyes were wild; his face was even paler than usual, showing up the five o'clock shadow on his chin as if it was painted on.

'I've been expecting you,' said my father, putting a forkful of sausage in his mouth, as calm as anything. 'How much will ye pay for the clock this time, MacClintock?'

MacClintock's eyes went to thin slits. 'I'll see ye in hell first,' he said.

'No,' said my father. 'I'll see *you* in hell first. That clock may be hell to you. But it rings like a cash-register to me. How much?'

'A hundred,' said MacClintock sulkily.

'I want a thousand pounds,' said my father.

'Be damned to you!'

'You're the one that's damned, MacClintock. Go an' get a good night's sleep. If you can.'

I don't know how much sleep MacClintock got that night, but I got none. The clock chimed and trumpeted every quarter-hour, and the sound seemed to fill the world. I tossed and turned, thinking of the heartlessness of the universe. In the sea, as I knew from biology lessons, the fish ate each other to live. And on the land, lions ate antelopes and fox ate rabbit. But I never realized before that men ate men. MacClintock gobbled up the poor and the foolish, and now my father was gobbling up MacClintock.

It was not love that made the world go round, as a popular song of the time said on the radio. It was money. All the world was reduced to how much will you give me, MacClintock?

As I imagined him tossing in his bed, I lost my hate of him, and began to feel pity. I felt pity for the three days and nights that followed. Pity and a mounting despair.

On the first day, he went to the village bobby. But the village bobby, when he came with him to our door, shook his head and would do nothing. MacClintock had smashed and abandoned the clock in the public domain, i.e. the back alley, and anyone could keep the bits . . .

On the second day, MacClintock turned up with two of his big debt-collecting men, who made the mistake of threatening my father. My father went beserk, and laid the two of them flat. And bloodied MacClintock's nose right in the middle of the street, in front of half the village.

And all the time, things screwed up tighter and tighter, like

117

a clock-spring over-wound. And I knew what blood could be spilt when a clock-spring broke.

The third evening, MacClintock came brandishing a shotgun. One that his bailiffs had taken from Tom Moreton, in payment of a debt. I don't think he meant to shoot anybody; I think by that time, he didn't know what he was doing. I think he was crazed with guilt, and lack of sleep, and the clock never stopping chiming and trumpeting outside his windows.

At the height of the yelling, the gun went off. Somehow, my father got the front door shut nearly in time; he only got a few pellets in his hand. After that, MacClintock seemed to go beserk, firing at all our windows. I remember lying across my mother to protect her, as the glass showered over both of us.

The noise fetched the village bobby. MacClintock took one look at the approaching uniform, and fled back into his house. The bobby demanded he come out and face the music; for the first time in his dreadful life, MacClintock found himself on the wrong side of the law.

It was the last straw. He fired at the bobby. And even though he missed, he knew then he would go to prison.

There were more policemen, all over the place, after that. They threatened MacClintock, then they pleaded with him. After about three hours (and still my father, in his white rage, kept the clock chiming and sounding) there was a dull bang inside MacClintock's house.

People said it was justice, that he killed himself with one of the last debts he ever collected.

Afterwards, I think I lived in a daze for a year. Though nobody in the village was sorry, everyone was very subdued. Hardly anybody understood the awful thing my father had done, except Tip. And Tip kept his mouth shut, and was very kind to me.

He had to be. I was in turmoil. How could a thing that I rebuilt for love have killed a man? Was that what the Major had meant, when he came to me in that dream, and said he had something else still to do? And was it really the Major, or only a dream? Nobody on earth could *ever* tell me.

But none of this ever bothered my father. Nothing interfered with the swing in his stride, the way he whistled as he set about mending a bridle, or banking up his potatoes. I could see no difference in him at all; except he would sometimes say regretfully that he wished he'd taken MacClintock's hundred pounds . . . He had no more regret in him than a fox that kills a rabbit, than a woodworm that makes a house fall. Than life itself.

In the end, I found I could live with him no longer. He destroyed all hope in me. So that when Tip got me an apprenticeship with an old clockmaker friend of his in Huddersfield, I left home thankfully and never returned. For all I know, my father may be living yet. And losing sleep over nothing. He was always a good sleeper.

When I left home, I took the clock with me. My father raised no objection. With MacClintock dead, he said, it was only a valueless curiosity. I have it still, in my shop. I have prospered, but never married. All the love I have to give is for my clocks; that they are rescued, and go back into the world, and give good service.

That, and the picture of Miss Gwendoline, which still sits, framed, on my mantelpiece. Beside the Red House clock.

Also by Robert Westall

THE SCARECROWS

While reluctantly spending the summer at his hated stepfather's house, Simon Wood takes refuge from the family pressures in the old mill house across the field. A discarded newspaper shows that it has been empty since 1943, but somehow Simon knows that there's more to the mill than meets the eye. Someone or something is watching and waiting, but for what? When the scarecrows appear Simon knows that its only a matter of time before he is faced with a terrifying test.

THE DEVIL ON THE ROAD

Pottering round the bit of Suffolk, where Chance and his Triumph Tiger-cub had landed him for the summer, John Webster found himself with a lot of unanswered questions. If he'd known the answers to those questions immediately, that little village wouldn't have seen him for dust. As it was, he had to find out the hard way ...

THE WIND EYE

Bertrand and Madeleine shouldn't have got married. Even their children seemed to think so – though they themselves got on as well as any half-brothers and sisters could be expected to. Their holiday together got off to a bad start when Madeleine trampled on St Cuthbert's tomb in Durham Cathedral, and from then on, the eye of the long-dead saint was well and truly on them ...

THE HAUNTING OF CHAS McGILL
AND OTHER STORIES

A rip-roaring collection of super-natural short stories, guaranteed to set spines shivering. They are full of vigour and excitement, tough humour and an appreciation of real people that sweep the reader along.

Also by Robert Westall

URN BURIAL

When Ralph discovers the mysterious creature buried beneath the ancient cairns high up on the fells he realizes instinctively that he has discovered something that possesses enormous and terrifying power. He is frightened – but why is it that he cannot leave the creature and its strange tomb alone? Forces far stronger than Ralph are at work and soon he finds that the earth has become a new battleground in an old conflict of races far superior to man.